16

Landlocked

Catherine Johnson

PONT BOOKS

First Impression—1999

ISBN 1 85902 664 8

© Catherine Johnson

Catherine Johnson has asserted her right under the
Copyright, Designs and Patents Act, 1988, to be
identified as Author of this Work.

This book is published with the support of the
Arts Council of Wales.

Printed in Wales at
Gomer Press, Llandysul, Ceredigion

Chapter 1

The blood came out in a rush and completely soaked through Iestyn's T-shirt. He felt it warm and sticky against his chest. What if it was his jugular vein, severed? Or worse, his aorta sliced open, throbbing out his blood. He felt very sick. Maybe it would be better to have died on impact. He shut his eyes. He could hear Richard groaning in the driving seat. They must both be alive. Iestyn could still hear his heart beating.

Slowly he felt for a wound, pulling the bloody T-shirt away from his body and brushing shards of windscreen onto the floor. His chest was whole. His hands went up to his neck. Nothing.

Richard next to him looked out through the remains of the windscreen to the massive pine a metre away. He swore, feebly.

Iestyn was still bleeding, he could taste it in his mouth. He wiped his face with the back of his hand and started laughing.

'It's a nosebleed!' He looked at Richard, relief washing over him. 'I thought I was dead!'

Richard ran his hand along the fractured plastic dashboard. He wasn't laughing. He folded his arms across the steering wheel and put his head down.

Iestyn held his nose, trying to stop the flow and pushed the passenger door open. He crouched with his head between his knees. His feet crunched on broken glass that was mixed in with the soft pine needles on the forest floor. The tape was still playing a mix tape Iestyn had nicked off his big sister and the tree was still creaking. Everything else was quiet.

When he felt the flow slowing Iestyn, unbent. The bonnet of the car had been stove in by a 6-metre scandinavian pine. The tree had been grazed and the smell of resin, like toilet cleaner, made his head swim. A coil of light grey smoke curled up from somewhere underneath the v-shaped bonnet. Iestyn thought of every film he'd ever seen.

'Rich, man! Get out of the car! Get out now!'

Cars exploded. All the time.

Iestyn could picture the orange fireball blowing out with enough force to shoot him into the trees. He saw the TV pictures on *Wales Today* tomorrow. He saw the newsreader with the shiny lips and the surprised eyes interviewing his tearful Mam at the kitchen door.

'He was a good lad.' Sniff. 'Halfway through his GCSEs. Had his whole life . . .' She broke down, hugging his sister, Rhiannon, who pushed the newsreader back through the door.

'Leave us alone. Now!' Rhiannon scowled. The newsreader was shaken, you could tell. She turned back to camera looking serious but concerned . . .

Iestyn pulled the blood-drenched T-shirt off over his head and felt the cold cool the wet, warm blood on his skin.

Richard needed help to get his door open. The

metal had concertina'd and the door was stiff. Iestyn pulled him out and Richard shook the fragments of safety glass off himself.

There was more smoke now. Even in the dark of the forest they could see it, smell it.

'I want the plates.' Richard could feel some cuts on his face and his legs were shaky but he was all right.

'I want the plates. That was my car. Dad'll kill me. He'll bloody kill me.'

'Look, Rich. It could go up any minute. Any bloody minute.' Iestyn wanted to start running. 'The force of the blast, man! Fifty per cent burns! Come on, man!'

Richard was close to tears, 'My car!'

Richard waited. There was no explosion. The tape slowed into alien-speak and stopped. The smoke fizzled out and the forest was still.

Richard wanted to start it up, to reverse it out of the tree.

'It'll work, Iest. At least if we can get it to the road . . .'

'Yeah? What? I can't see your Dad coming out with the tractor to tow us home.'

It wouldn't even turn over. Richard sat in the driving seat turning the key until at last the ignition didn't even click.

'Come on, Rich.'

Iestyn watched Rich wrench the back number plate off and they started walking.

'A965 GCC.' Richard held the plate reverently. 'I

was going to take my test in that car. Dad had booked it for September, after my birthday.'

Iestyn's trainers were full of pine needles. Richard didn't know he was born, having a car of his own.

'Ten more weeks and I would've been legal.'

It took fifteen minutes trudging through the trees to get to the road.

It was not yet dark and the road looked shiny even though it was dry, and it curved, lighter than the forest, over the rise and up to the moors.

Iestyn felt cold to his insides. He hugged himself.

'Let's hitch,' Richard said.

'No one's going to pick us up! We look like axe murderers!'

But there was no one on the reservoir road. It was only half past nine on a Friday night and totally empty.

'God, I hate this place,' Richard said.

Iestyn just kept walking.

They'd got around half way, just to where the table of the moorland begins to fall away, when a camper van, silver it looked in the dark, slowed after it passed them. Richard started running.

Iestyn caught up and saw the back of the van had stickers. Looked like hippies, he thought. The passenger door was open and Richard stood talking to the driver. In the light from the car, Richard looked like he'd just fought off wolves. Iestyn slowed and tried wiping any blood off himself.

The driver had hair so short Iestyn wasn't sure he

had any. He wore combat trousers, like a student –
only older, Iestyn reckoned. Hippy punk.

'You two had some trouble?' the man said, looking
at the blood.

'We had a smash . . . with the car. He had a
nosebleed.' Richard pointed at Iestyn. Iestyn looked
at the man. He didn't look like a nutter. The back of
the van wasn't fitted out for sleeping. There were
slim tree trunks, young pines from the forest, Iestyn
thought. And a bag of tools.

His T-shirt had a black man with a gun and words,
in seventies bubble writing: 'The Harder They
Come', it said. It was old.

'You sure you're alright?'

Richard nodded. 'Are you going through Cerrig?'

Stupid question, thought Iestyn. The road didn't go
anywhere else. Just down to the village where it met
the main road. No towns, no life for miles.

'Get in.'

Iestyn made Rich get in first. The driver told them
his name was Tony, didn't say much else. He clicked
on a tape with the volume up loud. Iestyn knew it
was Jimi Hendrix. 'It's what me Mam listens to,' he
said and the man laughed.

He dropped the boys off at the war memorial, a
stone girl holding a poppy wreath opposite the
Presbyterian chapel, and drove off towards Betws and
the mountains proper.

'Bye then, Mr.' Iestyn waved his bloody shirt after
him.

9

Richard cradled his car number plates in his arms.

'See you then.'

'Yeah, English on Monday.'

'No excuse for no revision now.'

'My Dad's going to kill me.'

'I'll come and help you with the car tomorrow.'

'Yeah, tomorrow,' said Richard.

Iestyn turned out of the centre of the village and towards the council houses this side of the big road. He was glad he didn't have to walk another half a mile to Richard's farm.

Iestyn pushed his front gate open. Pryderi, his younger brother was still up. He was standing in the front garden looking for aliens.

'Not been abducted yet, then?'

Deri didn't look up. He had a telescope on a stand that Gran had got him out of the catalogue last Christmas. And a book and a torch. Iestyn stood next to him and looked up. The sky had completely darkened to navy blue and it stretched starry and massive above the row of grey council houses.

'Piss off, Iest. You wait. Ten weeks, ten weeks. Then, when this comet shows up . . .'

'Yeah, Deri. I'll wait.'

'What happened to you?' Deri noticed the blood.

'Nosebleed.'

'And I was hoping you'd been savaged to death by a sheep.'

'Hah hah.'

Iestyn leant on the side door and wiped his feet.

Rhiannon, his sister, was in the kitchen on the phone, parts of her hair wrapped in little tubes of silver foil. No wonder Pryderi believed in aliens.

Iestyn put his bloody shirt in the washing machine and washed his face and arms. The warm water made his skin sting. He hadn't realised he'd got so cold. He pulled a clean shirt off the drier and opened the fridge door: a packet of salami, some cheese going off and what was left from a chicken his mother had cooked last Tuesday.

Iestyn pulled off a leg and took it through to the front room.

Mam was sitting in her chair reading a book. She still had her uniform on from work, a red nylon checky overall with a name badge, 'I'm LINDA here to help' in red letters. Iestyn hated that name badge. The fact that anyone who stopped in at the Laughing Chef for a nice cup of tea and a sausage and egg with two slices knew her name really annoyed him. Linda fiddled with her badge as she read. Her hands looked red and tired: 'working hands' she'd say. Iestyn swallowed. He hadn't told her about the job. Hadn't told anyone yet.

'What you reading?' Iestyn walked over to the telly and flicked it on.

Friday night clubbers in Birmingham waved their hands in their air.

'Hello, Iest. Oh, this? It's *The White Goddess*. It's *ever* so good.'

And she bent her head back over the book.

Richard's Mam liked cut glass animals and hard-eyed dolls in velvet frocks with names like Coretta and Jessamine. Any time she had not daubing the sides of sheep with turquoise spray, she spent dusting.

Linda Follett never dusted. She just sat around reading. When he was little and other people got outings to Chester Zoo or Alton Towers, Iestyn was dragged round burial mounds in Anglesey. Linda was seriously into mythology. That's why she'd moved up here from the midlands. That's why the children had such heavy names. Dad had never been happy about the names.

Iestyn plonked himself on the sofa, sinking into the hole between the cushions.

'Your roots are showing, Ma.'

'Rhi said she'd do them for me tonight. Rhi! Are you ready?'

'I'm on the phone!' Rhiannon shouted through from the kitchen.

'Only one more exam left, Ma,' Iestyn said.

'Oh . . . yes.' She bent the spine of the book to keep her place and put it down in her lap to show she was listening.

'Have you had any more thoughts about, you know, after . . .'

The way she said it, it sounded like dropping off a cliff.

'If you mean college, Mam, no.' Iestyn chewed his chicken. Maybe he should tell her, put her out of her misery. He smiled.

'I've got a job, Mam.'

Her face lit up. 'You're having me on, love.'

'Don't go mad, like. It's only one of them trainee things. Assistant Fishing Warden. Mr. Davies, at school, fixed it.'

Rhiannon came in, stirring a tiny pot of hair dye.

'I've got to be quick. Cerys is picking me up in ten minutes.'

'Listen, Rhi! Your brother's got a job.'

She raised her eyebrows, and the metal spike through her right eyebrow went up too. That was about as close to a smile as he got off his sister.

'Gonna make us rich, then?'

Rhiannon tucked a towel around her mother's neck and started dobbing the orangey gack out of the pot onto the dark brown of Linda's parting.

'It's only up the reservoir,' Iestyn said. 'It's only stupid trainee rubbish.'

'More than I've ever had.' Rhiannon dobbed a bit more.

She had been out of school two years now and had only ever managed a part time job in an old people's home and two weeks selling sheep's milk ice-cream in Llangollen for the International Eisteddfod.

Iestyn flicked the telly over. It was embarrassing, really. He didn't know the first thing about fish but he couldn't turn a job down. He might never get another one.

'There you go, Mam.' Rhiannon had finished. 'Don't forget, rinse it off in twenty minutes, and don't blame me if it doesn't work. Covers all grey – look! It says on the pack.'

Rhiannon went upstairs and came down again without the silver foil. Underneath, her hair was two-tone blonde. She wore a tiny T-shirt under a huge puffy jacket and a short skirt over bare, fake-tan legs that ended in trainers.

'You're going out. Now?' Linda looked upset.

'I said. Yesterday. Cerys has got the car. We'll be fine.'

'Where are you going, then?' Iestyn asked spraying tiny shards of chicken out of his mouth.

'Dance, over Bala. And no, you are not coming.'

Outside, a car horn beeped and Rhiannon left. Deri came in, dragging his telescope on its tripod like a dead animal.

Iestyn felt sick. He couldn't work out if it was the dodgy chicken or the prospect of working all summer instead of racing motorbikes up the mountain with Rich. He should have kept his mouth shut.

'You alright, Iest?' Deri stopped in the hall. 'It's brilliant out there tonight! I could see Venus and Saturn and the Pleiades . . .'

Iestyn made it to the kitchen sink just in time.

Chapter Two

Iestyn had a pile of English revision on the table in his bedroom. It was wedged beside the disembowelled TV that had stopped working after Christmas. It was never going to work now, not since Deri had taken the back off it. Snakes of copper coloured wire exploded out of it. Dust-covered microchips stood proud of circuit boards like old teeth.

Iestyn pulled the sheaves of paper free and lay down on his bed and looked at the top sheet; *Much Ado About Nothing*. Story of my life, he thought. Outside it was pouring with rain. Not the soft fine misty rain that just wetted you without knowing, but the hard, sideways driving sort that stung. Acid rain maybe. There was no way they could check out the car today.

The words in his English folder floated around in front of his eyes and Iestyn put the folder down. He had all weekend. Anyway, if he had a job now what was the point of exams? Exam. One left.

He went to his schoolbag and pulled out the letter. The letter about the job. He'd got it under false pretences. Last winter they'd all done work experience. Rich was lucky; he'd had two weeks at home helping his Dad. A few kids had landed jobs at the trailer company in Corwen, but there wasn't much round here – correction – wasn't *anything* round here. Iestyn had gone to the water board as an Office Junior. Every day to bloody Mold in a tie. He didn't know whose idea of a joke that was. Iestyn supposed that at least he knew he never wanted to work in an office ever again. All he'd done was fill the photocopier with paper and look at the office girls' legs in their shiny flesh-coloured tights. The letter said he'd been reliable and responsible, bright. He looked over the letter to his reflection in the mirror above the sink in the corner. His hair was a mess, not long enough to be floppy, not short enough to be hard. He looked pale. That must be loss of blood. Dead-eyed like the fish he'd soon be getting to know at work. Iestyn rolled back on the bed.

He knew as much about fish as he did about the meaning of metaphor in Shakespeare's plays. He wished he'd never told Ma about the job.

Downstairs the phone rang and Deri shouted up.

'Iest! Iest! It's Richard! Says you have to move his car or something!'

It took all day.

The forest was wet and the smell of damp pine hit you in the back of the throat. The ground was slippery with mud or shiny pine needles and Iestyn was soaked. The rain percolated down through the trees in large heavy drops that plopped down the back of Iestyn's neck and ran down his back. But by late afternoon, when they'd roped up the wreck and managed to turn it around, the sun came out. Tiny ribbons of light streamed down between the branches. Not ribbons, more like lasers, Iestyn thought, or strobes chopping the movement of Rich and his Dad into flickers. Iestyn thought it was better than a lot of the special effects they do on the telly. The light seemed solid.

'Iestyn! Bloody hell, you could do something! This is your mess!'

Richard's dad was seething. Iestyn stopped staring and started looking like he was doing something. Richard was as nervy as one of his sheep. Iestyn thought he was going to start bleating any second.

'Whose bloody stupid idea was it to take the car off the road?' Richard's dad yelled. 'I mean, it's an Escort not a bloody Land Rover!'

When they reached Ty'n y Fedw, Richard's dad stomped into the house without looking once at Iestyn.

The boys pushed the wreck into a barn. Richard stood still, staring at it.

'Rich, are you coming over mine tonight?' Iestyn asked. 'I've got the new Jackie Chan. My Dad sent it.'

Richard shrugged. 'I'm doing nothing. My Dad reckons I've got to pass exams before I start thinking about another car.'

'Oh.'

'Yeah, an' he's locked the quad bikes up and all. Except for work. He says I'm going to be doing a load of work this summer.'

Iestyn shook his head sympathetically. 'Me too.' Iestyn watched, Richard pulled the yard gate closed behind them. 'Up at the reservoir.'

Richard looked blank.

'You remember, after that work experience, when we made Deri fill in the . . . eval . . . evaluation form.'

Richard smiled, 'Yeah.' But Iestyn could tell he was still thinking about the car.

The track from the farm was half sheltered by wind-blown hedges; through the gaps the fields were treeless and bare. Walking home, Iestyn felt damp and cold. Dad had sent the Jackie Chan video with a letter. He said he was going to Spain in October with Natalie – his wife – and the baby. Dad had even asked if he would like to go with them. Iestyn hadn't said anything to Mum or Rhi. He kept it to himself so he could think about it without anyone going on at him.

Cai and Steff at school had been to Spain, said it was great. The beach, girls, women, topless and that. Maybe he didn't like the idea of Dad sunbathing next to a topless Natalie. Maybe that put him off.

By the time he got down to the village the lights in the pub were on but the car park was empty. Over the road in the church hall the Ladies of the Dawn were assembling for a treasure hunt. Under the bridge that crossed the little river that came down off the moor, Jonathan Mottershaw and some of Year 9 from school were drinking their mothers' duty-free Baileys. Iestyn smiled. Rhi's friends were outside the garage, sat in cars and playing tapes loud. He saw Rhi and her mate laughing, mouths wide open, but he couldn't hear them.

He speeded up. If he saved enough he could get a wreck, better than Rich's. His smile broke into a grin. Maybe a car *was* possible. Maybe the fish could do him a few favours.

He burst into the house where Deri was watching Stephen Hawking on the telly explain the mysteries of life and Quantum physics.

'Deri, Deri!' Iestyn had it all worked out. He was going to be the most excellent fishing warden in north Wales – no, Wales. He would be worth his weight in fish, they would up his salary and he would buy his own four wheel drive. Yes!

'Iest, go away.'

'Deri, listen. Just lend us your fish books.'

'You can have them for all I care, Iestyn. Now go away.'

Before Pryderi had discovered the stars he had been mostly into fishing with Little George next door. Now he borrowed armfuls of books from the mobile library about black holes and crab nebuli, the validity of time and Shroedinger's Cat. Maybe there was a Shroedinger's Fish lurking unknown in a clump of virtual pondweed at the bottom of a theoretical lake.

Iestyn bounded upstairs. He scooped the English revision papers off his bed and sat down with *Trout: The Queen of Fish*. After fifteen minutes he remembered Jackie Chan waiting to kung fu his way out of trouble downstairs in the video player.

Pryderi was still communing with Stephen Hawking.

'Come on Deri, I've got this video . . .'

'Haven't you got revision? Mum said you've got an exam on Monday.'

Iestyn slammed the door and sat down in the kitchen. The phone sat half way up the wall like the slugs that came in through the gap under the door in winter. There was no one to phone – they'd all be revising.

Work had to be better than this.

After the exam, school sort of fizzled out. It felt strange hearing Deri getting dressed, rushing for the school bus, while he lay still pretending to be asleep. Half his class were staying on at school. Sixth form; A levels, resits, NVQs. The other half were going to the FE college in Rhyl. Few had jobs.

Iestyn went in one last time to clear his things, pushing through the scratchy glass doors and onto the dirty lino in front of the office under the school council photos. He felt like a tourist in Hell. The bell went and hundreds of black-uniformed pale-skinned kids poured between one class and another. It smelt of feet and sweat and cheap sweets, Iestyn almost laughed, he'd already forgotten the smell. With every step towards his old class he knew he'd done the right thing. He'd had enough of this, of school. There wasn't much of him left here. A third of his life and no one would have known he existed. School had worsened during the last two years and it wasn't just the gearing up for the exams. It felt more like Deri's school than his.

Iestyn was anonymous, average – not like Rhiannon, who had bleached her hair in year 8, or like Deri who'd read more books than most of the teaching staff.

Mr. Williams, Careers, grabbed him in the corridor on his way out.

'Iestyn Follett!' Mr. Williams was wearing suede shoes and green trousers. Richard used to swear he was gay but then some girl in his class said she saw him kissing a woman, full on, outside the Eagle Hotel in Llanrwst.

'Mr. Williams?'

'I thought you'd be hard at it by now, Iestyn. When do you start?'

'Day after tomorrow, sir.' Iestyn stared at the tomato pip stuck to his tie.

'Well, I hope – we all hope – it'll be just the thing, Iestyn.'

Iestyn looked past Mr. Williams and into the school car park through the window. He could have sworn he saw Richard. But Richard had said he wasn't coming into school today. He said he was going to Denbigh with his dad to enrol on a course; 'The Cyberfarm: Selling Sheep by Satellite and the Internet.'

'Thanks, sir. Look, I have to be going.' Iestyn ran by him and down the corridor towards the stairs.

'You make the best of it, then.' Mr. Williams shouted down the corridor at him.

Iestyn ran down the stairs two at a time. He pushed through the door but couldn't see anyone. Must have been someone else, Iestyn thought, and he stood for a moment, catching his breath. Then he straightened, upturned the corner and almost walked into Richard who had his face glued to Martine Lloyd from Year 10 who had a smile like a basking shark and tiny eyes to match.

'Rich!' He hadn't meant to say anything, just walk past. But the word just fell out of his mouth. Rich disengaged. Martine Lloyd was grinning. Richard was sweaty.

'I forgot! I had to come in to school anyway! Pick up a letter about this course. Dad dropped me off!'

Iestyn felt embarrassed listening.

''S okay.' He started walking away.

'I'll give you a ring. OK?'

'Later.'

Iestyn walked out of the school gates. It would be a long wait for a bus. He stood there at the side of the road. He couldn't imagine Rich fancying Martine Lloyd. He didn't seem the type. Not that Martine Lloyd was Iestyn's type or anything. No way.

That wasn't to mean Iestyn had never had any girlfriends himself. There was Lisa Morris but he supposed she didn't really count because that was in

Year 7 when they'd just snogged a bit and held hands. Last year he made the mistake of dancing too close to Clare Price, drinking a couple of beers and asking her out. It was the worst date of his life. Her Dad drove them to the multi-screen in Wrexham and sat outside waiting for them in the car park reading a book about military strategy in the Crimean War.

Iestyn sat inside for two and a half hours waiting for some boat to sink and trying to kiss her. By the time the ship did hit the sea bed he'd gone right off the idea. After that he'd spent three whole weeks trying to work out how to tell her it was finished.

Before the exams he had seen a girl in Denbigh, at the swimming pool, and he'd thought about her for weeks. Still did sometimes. She had a black Speedo swimsuit with a racing back and she dived, arching up into the air, launching herself off the diving board and twisting round before hitting the water and floating up like a cork. Like a streamlined aerodynamic cork. Her back and arms were peppered with freckles. He didn't see her hair because she wore a blue rubber swimhat, but Iestyn imagined it red, or light brown.

Maybe she'd come swimming up the reservoir in the holidays and he would see her diving off the jetty. He smiled. The bus crawled into the bus stop and hooted at Iestyn to get on.

The day before he started work Iestyn went to Kwiksave in Corwen with Linda. He saw Richard in town, sitting in the sad burger bar with Martine. They were waiting for the bus to the cinema in Wrexham, Richard said. Richard said his dad was still dead angry about the car and Martine sucked her coke through a straw making a screwed up face as if she agreed.

Iestyn ran back into Kwiksave to find Linda but he got sidetracked by the open freezer cabinets. 'Fish', it said on the cardboard sign hung from the ceiling. Could be useful, he thought, as he peered down through the plastic stay-cold strips.

There were plenty of fish, but most of them had stopped looking like fish somewhere between the North sea and a Russian factory trawler.

They had been rearranged into interesting blobs, nuggets or goujons. Some had been spread with pizza sauce and all had been breadcrumbed. In the deli he managed to find some shrink-wrapped mackerel fillets that did look like they had once been part of a fish. He pulled them off their hook and stared hard at them.

'Iestyn, love, there you are. Will you not get a move on?' Linda pushed the trolley past him.

'I'm checking the fish, Ma.' The plastic was so shrink-wrapped you could see every ripple of fish flesh. 'So I know. For tomorrow.'

'Mackerel come out of the sea, Iest. Didn't they teach you anything?'

Iestyn hung the fish back on its hook.

'I know how you feel,' he said to the fish.

Chapter Three

The alarm had gone off half an hour ago and Iestyn was still asleep.

Deri was up already. School uniform on, working on his map of the stars on the floor. It was made out of A4 sheets of paper sellotaped together.

'Look, Iest, it folds out, see, and this line here . . .' He squeaked red magic marker between Mars and Venus, 'this line is the trajectory of the comet!'

The smell of the felt pen kicked inside Iestyn's head.

'Hell, Deri!' It was quarter to eight. He had fifteen minutes to meet his lift. He had to be in the warden's office at half past. 'Why didn't you wake me up earlier?' Iestyn swung his feet out of bed and landed somewhere in the asteroid belt.

'Watch your feet, Iest!'

Iestyn looked down at the stars. He could recognise some of the names: Orion, Pluto, Sirius, Saturn. He reached for his clean pants and dragged himself to the bathroom.

'Deri, I don't believe you are my brother . . . you were swopped at birth with an alien, from . . . Jupiter.'

'Don't be soft!' Deri shouted back. 'You know nothing, Jupiter is a gas planet! Nothing can possibly live on Jupiter. Io, that's a different matter . . .'

Iestyn pushed the bathroom door shut so he

couldn't hear him any more. In ten minutes he had to be stood at the junction of the Brenig road where Mrs. Hughes, who worked in the visitors' centre would pick him up in her dung-brown Vauxhall Cavalier.

Downstairs it was quiet. Rhi was still in bed and there was a note on the kitchen table from Mam, who was on earlies all this week.

'Iestyn, can in fridge, cheese for sandwiches, no milk for tea. See you tonight. All the best, love Mam.'

Iestyn picked up the note and stuffed it into his pocket. The letter from the Water people said they'd provide 'suitable workwear', so he'd put on his second best jeans and the T-shirt Rhi had got him in Chester for Christmas.

He picked up the lump of cheese and the back end of the loaf out of the breadbin, twisted them into an old Kwiksave bag and shut the kitchen door behind him.

Iestyn sprinted down the road and turned the corner past the post office. He could see Mrs. Hughes revving her car, sending puffs of black smoke out of the exhaust and onto a trough of geraniums that sat on the ground under the 'Welcome to Cerrig' sign. As he got to the car he could see there was someone else in the front seat already. He knocked on the back window and Mrs. Hughes flicked it open. Iestyn collapsed into the seat, breathing hard.

'I hope you're not going to make us late every morning, Iestyn Follett.'

'Sorry Mrs. Hughes.'

The girl in the front seat didn't look round. He knew who it was, though – his sister's best mate.

'This is Cerys,' Mrs. Hughes said. 'You remember Cerys ap Iwan?'

Iestyn heard the gears crunching as Mrs. Hughes steered the car out of the village. 'Cerys is just with us for the summer before she goes to University, aren't you, Cerys?'

Cerys said nothing.

'What is it you're studying?'

'Medicine, Mrs. Hughes.'

'That's it, medicine! All the way to London to be a doctor. Your parents must be so pleased.'

Mrs. Hughes looked at Iestyn in the mirror.

'And what's your Rhiannon doing nowadays?'

'Molecular Physics actually, Mrs. Hughes.'

'Pardon?'

Cerys stifled a laugh.

'Hairdressing. She does hairdressing, Mrs. Hughes. She's like a travelling hairdresser – in people's houses, doing their hair.'

Cerys opened her window and flicked out a blue ball of chewing gum. Iestyn caught her profile. She was grinning. She was mates with Rhiannon even though Rhi had left school and Cerys had stayed for sixth form. Her Dad was the vicar. Iestyn stared at the back of her head. How could Cerys ap Iwan be a doctor? He tried to picture her in a white coat looking concerned. A long flapping coat over her usual denim skirt and scuffed up Nikes. Racing along corridors holding those electric heart massage things. Turning off her bleeper and shouting, 'I need 5mls of adrenalin NOW!' at nurses. Tried to see her not chewing. Didn't work.

The road went up and levelled off at the top of the moors. Flatness for miles as far as you could see. On the horizon the outline of the ruined hunting lodge and the lump of some prehistoric twmp stood up to the right. To the left and straight ahead the road was enveloped in the pine forest.

The forest had been planted up on the moor not long before Iestyn was born. Linda said when she had come to Cerrig the trees were tiny, naked. Stood in rows like prisoners lining up for roll call. People complained at first, changing the environment, loss of natural moorland. But it was Crown land. It all belonged to the Queen, so she could do anything she wanted. There was this rumour at school about one of the wide flat moor mountains – Moels they were called – that one mountain was completely hollow. It was the Queen's bunker. If there was massive nuclear war, or even the hint of a small one in central Europe, she and her family and the corgis would land in their royal jet and lock themselves inside. Iestyn wasn't sure if he believed it.

Mrs. Hughes turned off the main road before she passed the crash site.

Iestyn watched the road slope down to the reservoir. Vast and flat and bright blue.

'Beautiful weather!' Mrs. Hughes steered into the car park. 'We'll be busting with visitors today, you'll see.' Cerys and Iestyn got out and Mrs. Hughes locked the car and started walking down to a large wooden building set into the slope at the edge of the water.

Suddenly the sky was filled with noise. Cerys didn't flinch. She'd lived with the jets all her life. Iestyn couldn't help looking, scanning the sky until they came into view. It was a good ten seconds before he saw it.

'Look!' Iestyn pointed across the water to where a black shape flew low and corkscrewed before heading almost straight up into the sky and off to the west. They came all this way to practise their low flying. Rich's dad complained about them scaring his precious sheep. Deri was sure they were hunting crashed UFOs. Everyone in the village was used to them.

Iestyn still loved them. He used to see himself as a pilot. Pinned into his seat with the G-force pushing his face around like putty. He'd fly dead low and pull up, just like that. Rich got a game for his N64 but it wasn't any good. Not like the stuff in his head.

He saw Cerys watching him sideways, like she thought he was mad.

'I, er, like the jets.' Stupid, stupid thing to say.

Cerys smiled at his complete lack of cool. She leant against the car, pulled a squashed packet of cigarettes from her bag and lit up.

'I thought you were going to be a doctor. Doesn't that kill you faster?' Iestyn asked.

Cerys dropped the lighter into her bag. 'All doctors smoke.'

Iestyn thought of Dr. Logasingam, his doctor. He chain-smoked foul-smelling filterless cigarettes. His skin was wrinkled and brown as dry peat.

'S'pose so.' He had to agree. Cerys didn't look at him. She was always like this. Terminally cool, Deri called her. She had totally ignored them both for the past ten years at least.

'Cerys! Cerys! Come and meet Irene. She'll show you the cafe.' Mrs. Hughes shouted up at them.

'See you, then.' Iestyn watched her go. She walked like Rhiannon walked, one foot almost in front of the other. He could see the muscles in her legs working away under the skin. He imagined girls practising after school. Practising walking and talking and holding cigarettes and not smiling at anyone younger than you. Then he realised Cerys and Mrs. Hughes had vanished into the building and he ran down the slope, swinging his arms.

Brenig Visitors Centre was written in two languages and braille. Cafe, Museum and Shop; Disabled toilet. Iestyn looked for the sign that said warden's office and walked around to the water side.

The lake reflected the blue sky and the far, unforested side was that greeny gold colour of moorland grass. It was so sharp and still and clean. The only sound was the water lapping against the jetty and moving the little boats moored along it.

The warden's office was opposite the jetty. On the

door hung a fish-shaped sign that said Open in English and Welsh. He breathed in and leant on the door, pushing it open. It was more like a shop than an office. There was a glass counter full of knives, hooks and coloured feathers; little packets of fishing line, thermos flasks and olive green hats. On the wall was a map of the reservoir and part of the forest. He stared at it, tracing the track Rich had driven up and the spot where the Escort had met the tree. He didn't hear Mr. Barass come in.

'Iestyn Follett!' Iestyn jumped. Mr. Barass was dressed head to foot in the same olive green colour as the hat for sale. He had a small moustache which stretched across his top lip as he smiled.

'Iestyn Follett!' He said it again and held out his hand.

'Mr. Barass?'

'Welcome, welcome.'

Iestyn shook hands with Mr. Barass. He tried to remember the last time he'd shaken hands with anyone. Mr. Barass let go.

'Well, well, so you're our trainee.'

Iestyn nodded.

'If you take this lot,' Mr. Barass handed him a pile of olive green clothes, 'and change in the gents, I'll give you a tour.'

Soon Iestyn was the same olive green. The trousers were weird, cut like what his mother would call slacks, but the waistcoat was excellent. It had a mass of velcro pockets like a photographer or a war correspondent off the telly. Iestyn took his food out of the plastic bag and velcroed it all into separate pockets. Then he pulled the rubber boots on and went outside.

Mr. Barass drove Iestyn round the lake in a Water Board jeep. Iestyn hung on to the roll bar like he'd seen people do in films. The narrow little road, new and shiny black, curved in and out of the dark forest. Richard would love this road, Iestyn thought.

Mr. Barass was talking about the growth of fish tourism, day licences, illegal campers and litter. Iestyn was enjoying the ride and wondering how long it would be before Mr. Barass gave him a go on the jeep. This job had definite possibilities.

By lunchtime Iestyn had hired out two fishing boats, sold three maps and eaten all the food he'd brought with him. He wandered up to the cafe past a nursery school picnic and some kids throwing stones as far as they could out into the water.

In the cafe, Cerys was concentrating hard, trying to fill a paper cup from one of those fizzy drink machines. She overfilled it and sprayed her white frilly apron with fluorescent orange stuff. Iestyn watched as she tried again, succeeded, and handed it over to an impatient mother.

'Haven't you got a straw?' the woman demanded.

Iestyn smiled. Cerys was trying and failing to stay polite. He walked up to the counter and asked for a Mars bar and the same fizzy stuff to wind her up.

'Wouldn't you rather have a can?' She plonked a can of coke down in front of him.

'I'm the customer. I thought I was always right!'

'Little brothers are always wrong,' she said and started serving the woman behind him. The can sat on the counter, frost melting off it until Iestyn picked it up carefully with the tips of his fingers.

He went outside and sat on a swing in the adventure playground. He took a drink from his can and swung a bit, making furrows in the bark chip flooring with his rubber boots. He saw Cerys come out of the building and lean against the wall. She lit up a cigarette and pulled off her paper waitress hat, combing through her hair with her free hand.

'Tough, is it, in the cafe?' Iestyn shouted.

'Yeah, but at least *I'm* not here for ever!'

Iestyn felt the ice-cold can freeze onto the skin of his hand. He looked out across the shimmering water. He didn't want to watch her any more.

By the end of the day Iestyn was knackered. He could feel the athlete's foot kicking in from walking about all day in rubber boots. On the way home Cerys sat in the front looking out of the window and Iestyn sat behind her looking out of the opposite one. Mrs. Hughes said something about the first day's work of your life.

At home he sat down in the kitchen nursing his feet.

'What's it like, then,' said Rhiannon, 'life as a wage slave?'

She wasn't really listening, she was painting her fingernails metallic acid green.

'Thrilling, Rhi, thrilling. I've sold fake insects, I've checked fishing permits and I've rescued two lads from Runcorn who got stuck in their boat in the middle of the lake.'

'I thought it was a reservoir.'

'Lake, reservoir, whatever. Make us some tea.'

'Make it yourself!' Rhiannon held her hands out, shaking them around as if she had pins and needles. Then she started on her toes. 'And your feet stink!'

'At least my toenails don't look like they're covered in psychedelic snot.' Rhiannon took no notice of him. 'Your mate Cerys is having a lovely time in the cafe.'

'Yeah, well. I'm going over there any second. She'll be able to tell me all the things you've been doing wrong.'

'Well, she wouldn't know about anything. She's stuck in that shop all day.' Iestyn pulled his socks back on.

Rhiannon made a face at him and slammed the door.

Iestyn thought about having a bath but he'd had enough of water for one day. Mum came in with Deri, both of them holding an armful of books. She beamed at Iestyn, still in his workwear.

'Look at you, Iest!' She put the books down on the table. They were nearly all hardback. Iestyn read the spines: *Standard Dictionary of Mythology*, *Folklore in N. Wales*. The usual subjects. Deri's were paperback: *Nebuli and other Phenomena*, *Mapping the Heavens*, and one extra thick hardback with the name of the new comet, Fassbinder-Hurley, in black letters. Linda saw him looking.

'Yes, these! Mrs. Roberts from the mobile library saved them for us.'

Iestyn had mixed feelings about Mrs. Roberts and the mobile library. He still couldn't bring himself to go in. He used to when he was younger. Up the little steps in one bounce to get his fix of Fireman Sam. Then there was the waiting for Mam as she chatted to Mrs. Roberts. And waiting. And waiting. It was Mrs. Roberts who started Linda on the reading. Books, obviously, but there were other things inside the mobile library. Little windows on the outside world; posters for the Open University, sheaves of leaflets in racks, learning for all, pottery courses with creche, Welsh for parents, Welsh for work, evening classes in Corwen. One day, nearly twelve years ago, Linda had picked one of these up and phoned the number that evening before Dad came in for his tea. Well, she told herself, Rhiannon was seven now and Iestyn nearly five, she had more time for herself.

Neil, Iestyn's dad, thought it was a good idea. 'Widen your horizons, love,' he said. He felt guilty that she'd never gone to college or university. She was a clever woman, he knew that.

So Linda signed up for Early Mythology and Landscape, Tuesday evenings, 7 'til 9, in the community centre in Corwen. Mrs. Roberts even gave her a lift.

Myrddin ap Nefydd took the classes in English and Welsh. He had dark brown unkempt hair and green eyes. Linda always said it was the eyes – Deri's got them too; otherworldly eyes. Myrddin ap Nefydd also had a wife and three children in Penmachno so, as Neil said – and as everyone in the little grey row of council houses heard – what in heaven's name did the both of them think they were doing?

Linda spent a lot of time talking to Mrs. Roberts and in the end Neil left. A few months later, Pryderi arrived. Iestyn never found out what happened to Myrddin ap Nefydd, but he hoped it was prolonged and nasty.

Iestyn watched his mother and Deri drop the books on the kitchen table, sit down and start reading. Maybe Deri should start looking for aliens closer to home.

'So I'm making the tea then?' Iestyn said. No one listened.

He filled the kettle and clicked it on. He heard his stomach rumbling and looked in the empty breadbin.

'Oh, Iestyn love, I did make it to the shops. Look!' Linda pointed to a blue plastic bag on the floor.

'And you'll never guess who we saw!' Deri looked up, grinning. 'Your mate Rich and that Martine whatsit from school!'

Chapter Four

Work was all right. It was hard to imagine that only a few months ago he'd been at school, hard to believe that life hadn't always been like this. Luckily for Iestyn there were really only two types of fish in the reservoir: brown trout and rainbow trout. He got to know them pretty well. He brought a couple home for Linda one time, wrapped them in foil like Mr. Barass said and cooked them in the oven with some parsley and a bit of butter. She was well impressed.

The money wasn't great. It was better than nothing, but Iestyn soon realised that a car was going to be a long time coming on his wages. The weather was getting better all the time too. Iestyn missed the motorbikes and his mates.

Cerys was a surprise. It started one rainy day when the sky was almost yellow grey and the reservoir pockmarked with raindrops. Iestyn had eaten his sandwiches on Mr. Barass's desk and had half an hour's lunch break to kill.

'Take a look over the museum,' Mr. Barass said. 'There's not much to see, except some kiddie's earbones in a jar . . .' He shivered thinking about it. 'Bronze age they are, not my cup of tea, but there you go.'

There wasn't much to see, he was right. There was a cut-away iron age hut, some sad-looking stuffed animals, a diagram of the valley before and after flooding and a giant plastic trout head, fishy mouth open ready to eat a fly.

Iestyn looked at the fish head for some time before he realised that the exhibit was supposed to be part of an underwater scene. There were giant green boots, like his own, part of some enormous fisherman who was supposed to exist somewhere above the imaginary water.

'Dump or what!' Cerys had come up behind him in her frilly apron and paper hat.

'I quite like this fish.'

'You've been working here too long then. Look at this paint job!'

She peeled part of the pink off its lip.

'Poor thing,' Iestyn said. Cerys made a face. 'You're forgetting I am Assistant Fishing Warden; it is my duty to protect all fish.'

'*Trainee,*' Cerys flicked a pinky flake of paint into the pretend reeds.

'Assistant Trainee.'

'Whatever.' She waved her hand dismissively.

Cerys said the other girl in the cafe, Brenda, was thick as two planks. She said it wound her up sometimes just looking at her. So some lunchtimes Cerys would come to find him and they'd sit together on the jetty, Iestyn dangling his sweaty feet in the water, talking. She was a different girl then, nothing like the one who stood in the doorway at home waiting for Rhi, staring at him with total contempt.

She talked to him about London.

'I tell you, Iestyn, I can't wait. This place is just doing my head in.'

Iestyn laughed. She looked at him. Her eyes were pale tobacco brown like the inside of her Silk Cut extra lites.

'Don't you want to get out? Don't you hate it here?' she asked.

Iestyn shook his head. ''S alright, I reckon.' He felt stupid for not wanting more. Cerys was staring out across the water; she wanted everything, he could tell.

'Once I hit London I'm never coming back,' Cerys said.

'Not even for holidays, Christmas?' Iestyn didn't mean to look worried.

'Not if I can help it. You know what I hate most?' she asked.

Iestyn shook his head.

'Everyone's so bloody minded, so small minded.'

Iestyn shrugged. He liked the lake and the moor, it didn't seem small to him. He thought of himself sitting next to her saying nothing, like an idiot, thinking so hard that he couldn't string two words together.

He shut his eyes for a second, tried to let go.

'It's just the people that are small and they're everywhere. You know our Dad, right, he lives in Telford. It's not so different there. More people, just all lumped in closer together. At least here we've got space.'

'Telford is hardly your cosmopolitan heartland though, is it?'

39

Cerys dabbled her feet. She had the same colour toenails as Rhiannon, only the green looked more goldish on her and less snot-like.

'I mean,' she went on, 'just today, just now, that Brenda! This bloke comes in, oldish bloke, scruffy – you know, earring and all.'

Iestyn nodded.

'Well, Brenda won't serve him. She stands there backing off from the counter like he smells. Which he does not. Whispers to me in that dead-behind-the-eyes voice of hers. "Don' like the look of him, Cez." So I go up, serve him. And he's nice as pie. Nice as bloody pie. Brenda was the same last week when we had that coachload full of orthodox Jews on their way to Bangor. Wouldn't serve them! Stared like a baby!' She rolled up her shirt sleeves to get more sun. 'That's what I hate.'

'Not everyone's like that, Cerys.'

'No, I know. It's not just that . . . it's . . .'

'It's no clubs and parties and clothes shops. You forget I live with Rhiannon.'

'Shut up, you.' And she kicked hard with her feet and splashed both of them soaking wet. Iestyn hadn't laughed so much since Rich almost drove into a cow in his back field. How could she want to get away from this, he thought.

Iestyn saw the hippy punk that afternoon. Mr. Barass had sent him over to the marina with a message and he walked down the road in the afternoon sun, glad his shirt was still wet with cold lake water on his back. He'd got around halfway when he saw the silver camper van, the one that he and Rich had a lift in after the crash. It was parked at the side of the road half in a ditch. It was empty. Iestyn walked around it calling 'hallo' but no one came. On his way back it was still there and the back door was open. Inside there were bits of wood, not whole tree trunks but large branches a metre long, and plastic bags almost bursting with pine cones.

Iestyn felt a thud between his shoulders as someone slapped him matily on the back. 'It's the Berwyn bloodbath boy!'

Iestyn turned round suddenly. It was the man – the hippy – carrying a bundle of twigs and grinning at him.

'What?'

'Joke,' said the man. He put his hand out. 'Tony, remember? I gave you and your mate a lift. You look clean.'

'Yeah, I try not to have too many nosebleeds. I'm working here.'

Tony put the twigs down in the van. 'Lucky man!'

'Is it OK for you to take this stuff?' Iestyn felt embarrassed for asking, but he didn't want to lose his job. 'I mean, have you asked someone?'

'It's cool,' Tony said, slamming the van door. 'I'm doing a job with the forestry people.'

Iestyn didn't really believe him and Tony must have seen it.

'Don't worry so much. You might get another nosebleed.'

Tony opened the driver's door and climbed in. He scrabbled in the glove compartment and pulled out a creased business card. 'Look.'

Iestyn looked. It read: *TONY CULLINAN Pyrotechnician and Artist.* Iestyn was just thinking about what that might mean when he realised the camper van had started up and was heading down the road.

That afternoon Iestyn stood leaning against Mrs. Hughes's car waiting for his lift. The car was parked almost under the trees and Iestyn wasted time kicking the pine cones as far as they'd go. Cerys walked up, shaking her head.

'If it's round you'll kick it. You're all the same!'

'I am not!' Iestyn smiled. He knew she was just teasing. 'I saw that bloke again.'

'So?' She turned towards him, shielding her eyes from the sun.

'He gave us a lift a couple of weeks ago, me and Rich – after we'd crashed Rich's car in the forest.'

'Your mate Rich the young farmer?'

'Yeah.'

'In the forest up here?' Cerys's eyebrows went up. 'Rhi never said.'

'I never told her.' Iestyn managed to kick a pine cone up off the floor and right into one of the rustic-look bins. 'Mam would've given us a shouting and Rhi would have stood there all smug.'

'I heard the story someone had come up here, mashed up a car. I didn't know it was you!'

'Ask Rich's dad. On the other hand, don't. He had to come and tow us out the day after. He wasn't too pleased.'

'Cool.' She smiled. 'I bet that was a blast, driving through the trees.'

'Blast is the wrong word,' Iestyn said. What he thought was, actually we were both shitting ourselves, but that didn't sound like such a blast.

He kept his mouth shut. Cerys looked into the forest then at him. She looked right at him, not through him or around the side of him or just off past the top of his head. Mrs. Hughes walked up the path. Iestyn tried not to smile too much.

The drive home seemed to take less time than usual. He didn't even realise when the car had stopped.

'Iestyn. Iestyn! You can get out now!' Mrs. Hughes said.

Iestyn jumped up and slammed the door after him. He watched the brown car turn left away from him and just before he started walking he saw Cerys. She was waving.

Chapter Five

The first morning of August, Iestyn woke up suddenly. In his dreams a half second ago he had been kissing her, Cerys, at work – she was in her frilly apron. They were in the museum in the visitors' centre pressed up against the giant dummy trout. Outside, above the reservoir, comet Fassbinder-Hurley was corkscrewing low over the water, an orange ball of flame speeding towards the building, faster than the speed of sound. Somehow, through Iestyn's dream senses, he was aware of both the comet and the tip of Cerys's tongue at exactly the same time.

Once he realised he was awake he tried shutting his eyes and forcing himself back into sleep but it was no use. The dream had gone. Iestyn looked across at Deri, still asleep and dreaming of galaxies and gas giants. He'd been up late last night watching a TV programme about the possibilities of the comet crashlanding into the earth. Some scientist reckoned it was the end of the world. Iestyn smiled and got dressed for work.

Linda was in the kitchen in her dressing gown reading a letter.

'What is it, Mam?' Iestyn made her a fresh cup of tea.

Linda looked up at him, pushing her hair away from her face.

'This.' She put the letter down on the table and pushed it across to him.

Iestyn saw the blobby chef-in-a-hat letter head. It was Linda's work people, a letter from the head office in Retford, wherever that was. 'We regret to inform you . . . due to falling custom . . . the impending closure of the Cerrig branch . . .' They were letting her go, it said, in a month. They were very, very sorry.

'Oh, Mam.'

Linda looked tired. She went to Rhiannon's bag hanging on the back of the door, rummaged around and pulled out a pack of cigarettes.

'Come on, don't start on that. I'll make you some toast.' Iestyn turned the grill on.

'You don't want to be late for work. Looks like you'll be the only one left in this house with a job.'

'Mam!'

Iestyn watched her light up, the smoke curling round her face. She looked grey and old. He didn't want to see her like this. He gave her a hug and left early for work. It would be easier not to think about it once he was out of the house. Easier to think about Cerys.

'Feels funny, not being at school, not having to go back to school. I was there for seven years,' Cerys sighed. 'Seven years.' She was leaning against Mrs. Hughes's car having her first cigarette of the day.

'I wish you wouldn't do that,' Iestyn said. 'That's my Mam, that is.'

'Saves me eating.'

45

Iestyn sighed. 'I could blow you over, there's so little of you.'

'Oh yeah?' She stared at him. 'Dare you, then.'

Iestyn blushed and turned away so she wouldn't see, started walking down to the warden's office.

'That's for kids, daring!'

'That's what you think.' Cerys shouted after him.

That lunchtime he walked with her up into the trees because he'd promised to show her where they crashed the car. Somehow, sometime she had stopped being the girl his sister went around with, the sullen shadow next to Rhiannon who always put him down. They just talked and talked. Rubbish mostly. He ended up singing the theme tune of Scooby Doo at her because she said she couldn't remember. She told him about the worst film she had ever seen which she said her dad loved. It was about two people who fall in love and don't do *anything* – just stare longingly at each other for an hour and a half at a railway station. He told her about sitting through some Armenian (Yes, he said, he was sure it was Armenian) film with his mother in Birmingham. And in fact, he said, even though he fell asleep, there were some good bits.

Cerys laughed. 'No! Serious!'

She had to believe him. There was this really good bit when these sheep came over the hill like a wave of whiteness.

She laughed more when he told her that. 'Of course you liked it – it's got sheep, and you're Welsh!'

Iestyn said, 'No, I'm not, I just live here.'

'That's the same thing.'

He found the tracks where they'd driven in and where Rich's dad's tractor had come to pull them out. They could hear the sound of sawing.

'Quiet!' Iestyn sshhed Cerys. 'It might be Forestry.'

Cerys wanted to go back. Iestyn smiled and kept walking.

It wasn't Forestry: it was Tony. He was wearing an eyeshield and carrying a chainsaw. He had cut down the tree Richard had crashed into and was sawing it into neat little log sections, like the ones for sale in bags outside the Laughing Chef. He turned the engine off when he saw them, pulled off his visor.

'Look at this,' he said. 'Some idiot killed this tree.'

Cerys giggled, but Iestyn felt guilty.

'It was us, me and Rich, the night you picked us up.'

'You should have seen them,' Tony said to Cerys. 'They were bloody and semi-naked. This one,' he pointed at Iestyn, 'was so white he glowed in the dark. A pair of nutters.' He shook his head. 'I suppose we have to be grateful they weren't on the road.' He smiled at Cerys and put his hand out to shake hers. 'Tony,' he said.

'Cerys.' She smiled.

'You work in that cafe, don't you, by the reservoir?'

'Yeah, just for the summer.'

'Me too.'

Iestyn hadn't thought too much about what Tony was doing. He imagined Tony was part of some tribe of hippies in bust-up lorries, moving around. There'd been some last summer up at the ruined hunting lodge on the moors, playing loud music all night. You could see the fires for miles.

'I'm an artist. The Arts Council of Wales and the Forestry have kindly given me permission to torch some of these trees.'

'What!' Iestyn looked alarmed. Perhaps the bloke was a nutter.

'He's worried about his fish,' Cerys explained. 'Being trainee fishing warden and that, he's scared the water might boil up or something.'

Cerys smiled again. Tony smiled back.

'Controlled burning. I make sculptures and set them on fire. I'm cutting this tree you knocked down for fuel, to go inside one of my models,'

'Great,' said Iestyn. What was the point of making something, he thought, and then wrecking it?

'Iestyn wouldn't recognise art if it hit him,' Cerys said. She actually looked interested.

'Didn't I give you my card, the other day?' Tony was stuffing another bag with the logs.

'Oh, yeah,' Iestyn nodded. It was still in one of his velcro pockets in his waistcoat somewhere.

'I'm setting everything up for the end of September. I don't know exactly when yet, depends on the comet.'

48

'The comet?'

'Yeah, the work's supposed to like, mirror the comet. Sort of millennial. Post-millennial really . . .' Tony suddenly looked like Deri drawing his path through the stars.

'I bet you weren't allowed to play with matches when you were a kid!' Cerys said.

'Why don't you two come over, maybe Saturday? Not too early: it has to be dark. I'm doing a sort of dummy run – you can get the idea. If you're interested, that is.' Tony looked like he'd feel hurt if they weren't.

Cerys nodded. 'That'd be great.'

Iestyn looked sideways at her. Since when had she been an art fan? She nudged Iestyn in the ribs 'We'd love to come, wouldn't we?'

'S'pose so,' Iestyn said.

Iestyn was quiet on the way back to work. She was fizzing. 'Look at the light through the trees, Iest! Isn't it great?'

'S'alright.' She wasn't interested in him. He had made it all up – wanted it so badly he thought it was real. She was more interested in that hairless ancient bloke than him.

'What's up with you?' Cerys asked. They stepped out of the forest and onto the lakeside road. Iestyn brushed the swarms of midges away from himself.

'That bloke, that artist. Look, I'm not sure if I want to spend a whole evening watching him set fire to stuff.'

49

'Not even if I take you for a drive on the way back?' Cerys said.

Iestyn stopped. Inside, his heart had speeded up to bursting.

'Well?' Cerys asked. Brenda was waiting in the car park.

'Cerys! There you are! Mrs. Hughes is going to kill you.'

Cerys broke into a run and caught up with Brenda. Iestyn watched the girls go in then he walked round to the warden's office. Mr. Barass was leaning across the counter demonstrating the different uses of the 'Easikill' dual-purpose gutting and scaling knife to two off-duty policemen from Chester. Mr. Barass, Iestyn thought, I could kiss you.

Chapter Six

The mirror in the bathroom was wrong. It was pitched the right height for Linda and Rhiannon, but six inches too low for Iestyn. He bent down and tried brushing his hair forward, and then back. He did that twice before settling on back and checking his skin.

Rhiannon had these weird white gummy strips that you stuck to your nose for half an hour and when you pulled them off all your blackheads came out like upside-down little worms. Iestyn read the instructions but it sounded medieval, like torture. Then he remembered the mammoth spot resting on his left shoulder blade. She wasn't going to be seeing that, but what if she held him, what if it got to the point where she's standing there with her hands up his shirt. He stopped. Don't count your chickens. He forgot the spot and put on the T-shirt Rhiannon said he looked almost human in.

'Where are you off to then?' Rhiannon leant against his bedroom door.

Looking at her Iestyn was reminded of one of the evil pond-dwelling spirits from his mother's mythology books.

'Out.'

'With a girl?' Her eyebrow went up.

'No, with a tame tortoise. What do you think?'

'Touchy!' Rhiannon scrutinised her indigo fingernails. 'Well, little brother, so long as you've cleaned around your neck and behind your ears.'

Iestyn swore at her and slammed the bedroom door in her face.

He was clean, though. Every inch. Rhiannon smiled as Iestyn left the house and Iestyn wasn't sure he liked the way she was smiling.

He thought about this for nearly ten minutes: what had Cerys said to Rhi? How much did she know? But by then he had reached the War memorial and there was Cerys sat in the driving seat of her mother's beat-up Talbot Samba. Everything was fine.

'Sorry about the car,' Cerys said. 'Hasn't even got a radio.'

Iestyn shrugged. 'So long as it goes,' he said and Cerys started up and headed for the moors.

She was wearing the usual denim skirt and Iestyn tried not to look down. The worst thing was when she changed gear and the back of her hand ran down the side of his thigh. She really didn't know, thank God, what he was thinking. Iestyn smiled a soft stupid smile at her and looked purposefully out at the curving road ahead, trying desperately to think of something to say that didn't have anything to do with legs.

Tony was staying in a cottage halfway over the moors to Llanrwst.

Cerys turned off the main road and onto smaller and smaller side roads until Iestyn was sure she was lost. He didn't mind, though. He could have driven around with her all night. She smiled at him, laughed when he told her about Deri's quest for life in the tail of Fassbinder-Hurley. But she was nervous, edgy. Iestyn quite liked that. He used to think she was too cool to feel.

They found the cottage eventually. It looked as if it had been two cottages once but one of them had become derelict and sloped off into an abandoned orchard of stunted apple trees. Outside the lived-in cottage was the silver camper van and a curvy old sports car, pale blue like Iestyn's mother's talcum powder box. It was a Jaguar: Iestyn recognised the silver cat on the bonnet. It was like something he'd seen on the telly.

'Now that is art.' Iestyn walked around it once.

Cerys nodded. 'Wouldn't mind that myself.'

The lights in the house were on and music was playing inside, coming out through the open windows. Iestyn always liked music outside; somehow the fresh air made anything sound better, even cheesy old people's music like this. It was reggae, Iestyn thought, recognising it off some advert.

'Hello!' Tony answered the door and let them in.

The walls were not painted weird swirly purple and yellow like Iestyn had imagined. It was more like the holiday cottage Richard's dad had for visitors: white walls and prints of castles in gold frames.

But instead of castles the pictures on the walls here were photographs mostly. Iestyn peered at them. In one there were these leaves frosted with white, pinned in a circle. In another there were icicles – real frozen natural, icicles – like a halo hanging above the ground from a tree. Each photograph was different: twigs arranged in spiral shaped waves; a maze made out of peat and turf.

'That's what I did before I discovered burning stuff,' Tony said.

Iestyn liked it.

'Is it art?' he asked.

Tony laughed. 'Course it's bloody art!'

Cerys laughed too. Iestyn felt bad. He thought of school and of the art teacher, a woman with a mouth too small for her head, going on about perspective.

'No, what I meant was I don't like art, like. I like this, though.'

There was a room with two sofas and a dark-skinned black woman loading film into two large black cameras. Tony said her name was Connie. Tony got them each a bottle of cold beer from the fridge and took them out to the derelict cottage next door. In between the trees there was a wooden structure on the ground, like a prone Catherine wheel made of pine branches.

'You're going to set fire to that?' Cerys asked.

'Yeah, I want to make sure it burns at the right speed and everything. Too fast and it's all over before you know what's happening, too slow and nobody "gets" it.'

'Like sex you mean,' Connie said. She had followed them out of the house and was already taking photos with a flash because the sky was darkening.

'There's no point waiting for Steve and Nicky, the Citroen broke down outside Shrewsbury,' Connie shouted across to them.

Tony picked up a petrol can from inside the derelict house.

'This is the bit I like.' He grinned at Iestyn and Cerys. 'I'm just a twisted firestarter,' and dropped a match onto the tail of the spiral.

Connie clicked furiously, Iestyn felt the heat of the flames on the skin of his cheek and arm. The dark trees in the orchard all reflected orange and the flames crept along the spiral of twigs crackling and popping. The air smelt of burning pine. After five minutes there was a perfect spiral curtain of flame.

'Excellent,' said Iestyn.

Connie was up a stepladder taking more pictures. Tony was running round with two of those garden water-squirters in his hands to damp down bits that were burning too fast. They stayed out watching it for ages. Even when the flames had died away the core of the shape glowed red.

'Let's have another beer!' Tony was ecstatic. When they got back inside he was glowing too.

'How d'you reckon it'll look, Con?'

Connie sipped her beer. 'Great, Tone, great. I'll have the prints for you next week.'

'Did you like it, then?' Tony asked them. Iestyn could only think of thickhead one-word answers. 'It's going to be down by the lake, in the dark. It's gonna work, isn't it?'

'Brilliant, bloody brilliant. Better than all those bonfires we get on the playing fields on Guy Fawkes. And that's your job!' Cerys was amazed. 'I'd die for a job like that!'

Tony sat on the edge of one sofa grinning. 'Well, that's me well pleased.' He lifted his beer: 'The Arts Council of Wales!'

'I cannot believe you make a living at that!' Cerys sank back into the white sofa. 'Here's me off to study for four years and you spending your life mucking around with twigs!'

Connie and Tony grinned.

'We are poor though, aren't we, Con?'

'Poor but happy,' Connie said, the black camera open on her lap as she took the film out.

Iestyn shook his head. 'You can't be poor and happy. It doesn't work. Poor and miserable, poor and bored, poor and . . .'

'He's right, y'know,' Cerys said. 'That's why I'm going to medical school. I don't want to spend my life like my mother. Making cakes for *Merched Y Wawr* and driving old ladies around. I want to have a place of my own and clothes that cost more than my dad earns in a week . . . a month!'

Cerys was driven. Looking at her, Iestyn could see she really did want all that. It made him a bit sad but Connie and Tony were on the verge of laughing and he didn't want them laughing at her either.

Connie poured herself another drink. 'So what are you doing then, Iestyn?'

Iestyn thought she sounded like Mrs. Williams the deputy head. He smiled and shrugged at her.

'I'm fishing warden.'

'Trainee,' said Tony.

'So you're the only one in this room with any kind of a proper job?'

They talked about London and Cerys was like a hoover scooping up bits of information. Tony said he had a studio in Hoxton. Cerys knew where it was.

'I love the A-Z,' she said.

'What is this girl on!'

Tony said he'd move out of London soon. Said he'd like to live somewhere like this, but he'd need to make a bit more money first and Cerys laughed at him then because she said that that proved her point. She said he wouldn't want to live here, poor, and Tony sort of agreed. Then Tony said he'd rather make money by setting fire to twigs than opening people up and sewing them together again. Cerys said she fancied doing plastic surgery.

'Then I can always get myself sorted when I get old,' she said.

'How old's old?' Connie asked.

'Old as us!' Tony said. 'Old as the hills.'

Iestyn felt out of his depth, like the plastic trout in the visitors' centre. He kept opening his mouth then shutting it again when he'd forgotten whatever it was he was going to say. Cerys could cope with anything, talk to anyone. He envied that.

Tony turned the record over and it was a tune Iestyn had heard before.

'I like this; Toots and the Maytals,' he said.

Cerys looked impressed that he knew something so specific. Tony offered to lend him a tape.

Connie started packing her camera up. She said she was going to a dinner party in Blaenau Ffestiniog. 'Are you two off to dance all night in a field? Isn't that what you're supposed to do these days?'

Cerys looked sideways at Iestyn, 'Nah, he's too young. But I suppose we ought to go too.'

Tony went outside with them. 'See,' he said, breathing in deep. 'This is what you'll miss, Cerys. Clean air, big skies.'

Connie kissed Tony goodbye, the sort of cheek-kissing Iestyn had only really seen on TV. Then she kissed Cerys and came straight for him.

'I'm sure she'll miss you too,' Connie said.

Iestyn looked shellshocked. Cerys giggled.

'She thinks we're like, together, you know,' Cerys whispered in his ear and the warmth of her breath made him shiver. He blushed.

Cerys giggled and slipped her arm around his waist. Iestyn thought he'd burst. He couldn't bear to move in case she moved and he ruined it all.

Connie started up the powder-blue Jag and drove away. Tony had already got some kind of welding goggles on. 'I'd better start earning money,' he said. 'Thanks for coming.'

He invited them to the official opening. 'It's not so

much an opening because it all depends on when the comet arrives. Anyway, see you there.'

Iestyn couldn't say anything and the quiet in the car was killing.

Whatever atmosphere or feeling there had been had evaporated and Iestyn didn't know why. Did his breath smell? Had she remembered he was her best mate's little brother?

He began to think he'd imagined her whispering in his ear. He put his hand up to check but the moistness of her breath had gone. She wasn't interested and they'd be back in village in twenty minutes. He had to do something.

'You said I could have a drive . . . remember, yesterday.'

Cerys thought. 'Not on the road, though. My Mam would kill me, OK?'

'We could go up Plas Bren, there's a track there.'

Cerys shook her head. 'That place gives me the creeps.'

'The reservoir, then. In the car park.'

Cerys nodded. 'So long as you don't drive us in.'

Iestyn had never been at the reservoir at night. It was very quiet, as if the trees absorbed any noise. There was the oily lapping of water beyond the visitors' centre, but that was it.

They swopped seats and he started up. He pushed it into first and he felt her leg against his hand and crunched the gear.

'Careful!' Cerys did not sound impressed.

After three uneventful circuits of the car park Iestyn asked if he could take it out on the road round the lake.

'It's not real road, it's private.'

Iestyn drove to the far side of the reservoir where the forest gave out to moorland. He started slowly and sped up over the hills so the car jumped and his stomach hit the floor.

'Shame there's no radio,' Iestyn said. He was almost too busy enjoying himself to remember Cerys was there. The last time he'd had a good long drive it had been in Rich's Escort up in the back field and not on a tarmac road like this. He liked the way the grey road came up towards you and turned and dipped over ridges and hills. He did a complete circuit and parked up in the car park.

'Thanks.' He was smiling now. Maybe he'd never get to kiss her but at least he'd driven her car. They both got out and Cerys lit up.

'Can't smoke in the car. Mam'd smell it,' she said.

Iestyn walked down to the jetty in the dark and took his shoes off.

The sky was that dark navy blue and there were more stars than Deri knew names for. Iestyn peeled his socks off, sniffed them – not too bad – and dipped his feet into the black water. It was tingling cold at first then he kicked his feet slowly, watching the shape of the shine on the water change. It was almost as good as the flaming spiral.

'Iest! Iest!' Cerys shouted from the car park then he saw the bright red dot of her cigarette come floating towards him, jumping down the steps by the side of the visitors' centre.

'Look!' The orange red dot went up and Iestyn looked up with it into the sky. It was a falling star, like a piece of pale ember thrown up and rushing down again, very far off.

'Where are you, Iest? Can you see the star?'

'I'm on the jetty,' he called back and she walked towards him out of the dark.

'Wasn't that amazing? Are you paddling? Isn't it cold?' She sat down cross legged next to him.

Iestyn splashed her. Cerys squealed and suddenly pushed him off the edge into the reservoir.

'You idiot!' Iestyn was flailing around in the water. It wasn't that deep but he was soaked.

'Look, I'm sorry. Iestyn, are you alright? Where are you?'

She sounded worried. 'Iestyn?'

Iestyn waved his arm towards her and she caught him, her arm skin all along his, her hand round his upper arm, her hand near his BCG scar.

'Come on, Iest.' She pulled, crouching in her trainers. Iestyn couldn't resist it. He stepped back, not forwards and pulled her on top of him.

'Iestyn!'

He felt her close as they hit the reservoir bottom then surfaced again.

They both stood chest high in the water

spluttering. She pushed him over and under the water and they came up again together. She was holding onto him, both hands gripping his waist. They laughed, ducking each other again and again until she pulled his face nearer. Iestyn shut his eyes ready for a smack or a splash and she kissed him. Full on.

Iestyn had never swum in the reservoir. He had watched little kids on the hot days after the schools had closed, even watched their Mums and Dads sometimes. But there was something about moving through the water in the dark, in blackness above and below. Parting it with the tips of his white hands and hearing the splosh as he moved through the water. He didn't feel cold, there was Cerys next to him her white bum sticking out of the water like two marshmallows.

They fell asleep on the back seat covered with Mrs. ap Iwan's travel rug. When the light forced him awake Iestyn moved his arm from under Cerys and walked barefoot over the pebbles to where they'd left their clothes. Everything was wringing wet, especially the trainers like dirty old sponges. It seemed much colder than the warm night before.

It was only half past five. Two hours until the weekend warden, Mr. Bishop, showed up.

'No one'll see us if we get back now.' Cerys wasn't phased or embarrassed. Inside he thanked her for that. His mouth ached from kissing, and his neck from sleeping curled up unnaturally but he felt great.

The hardest things were putting on the soaking

clothes. Cerys drove as far as the main road wrapped in the blanket. Iestyn sat in his jeans as stiff and heavy as wet board.

She dropped him off at the first crossroads outside the village, kissing him lightly on the cheek as if they'd just met.

He walked uncomfortably down the hill towards his house. The Edwards' dog at the end of his terrace started howling and Iestyn howled back.

Chapter Seven

'and the comet has a three in one billion chance of actually colliding with some part of our earth . . .'

'I think we have to be prepared for some repetition of those events some years ago . . . millennial fever . . . mass suicides . . .'

Iestyn rolled over. Pryderi had turned the radio on to listen to some old men and a young woman debate the implications of Fassbinder-Hurley. It was eleven-thirty. He pulled the pillow over his face and rolled over. He was back in the water with Cerys. Then he was out of the water under the travel rug in the back of the Talbot Samba feeling her skin pressed against his. Iestyn sighed. He re-ran all of last night from the moment he'd seen her sitting in her car until she dropped him off at the edge of the village. Some bits made him shiver just remembering.

On the floor, Pryderi was adding to his map of the stars. On the radio the young woman pointed out that the best view of the comet would be in north-west Europe and that Fassbinder-Hurley had never been seen by the naked eye and wouldn't be again for another five thousand years.

'Five thousand three hundred and eighty nine.' Deri corrected out loud.

Iestyn opened his eyes.

He had a bath that lasted an hour and found his mother in the kitchen. She had a bag of frozen croissants she'd bought home from work. Lots of stuff came home with her from work nowadays. Iestyn was getting fed up with Laughing Chef Mini Kievs or Gamm'n-Ham-'n'-Pineapple steaks. He didn't mind the croissants, though, and pulled one out of the bag and stuck it in the still warm oven.

'Mam!' He kissed her on the cheek.

'Is that so I won't have a go at you for being out so late? I went to bed after twelve and you still weren't back.' Linda had nearly finished *The White Goddess*.

'I'm sorry, Mam. I was out with Rich.'

'Rhi said you were out with a girl.'

'There was a few of us.' That was sort of true, Iestyn reckoned. 'There's some bloke doing sculptures on the moor. We watched a trial run. It was alright, as it goes.'

'Anthony Cullinan?'

'You've heard of him?'

'Look, he's in the paper. He was on the news last week, said he was doing something to celebrate Deri's comet.'

'He was on the news?'

'He does nice nature things with leaves and icicles and shapes and stuff.'

Iestyn watched his mother chewing a liberated Laughing Chef croissant.

'You've heard of him? Really?'

She folded the newspaper down. 'I said, didn't I?'

Iestyn should have known. Linda always knew more than she gave away. She marked the page of her

65

book and put it in a Kwiksave bag along with her glasses case and some real dairy Danish slices. She was going over to Mrs. Roberts's who ran a reading circle on the third Sunday of every month.

Iestyn tried hard not to phone Cerys up. Her Dad would be in church by now and he pictured Cerys in the bath. Iestyn put his naked feet on the kitchen table and drank his tea.

'What'you doing, Iest?' Rhiannon had surfaced. 'Tell Mam when she gets back I'm just over Cerys's doing her hair.'

Iestyn managed not to spill his tea.

'Doing what to her hair?'

Rhiannon grinned a wicked grin. 'What's it to you, little brother?'

He shrugged, hoping nothing showed. But Rhiannon was still looking at him too hard.

Iestyn watched her go up the path to the gate, swinging her Superdrug bag. They would talk. That was girls. They would dissect everything and look so hard at it that whatever had really happened would change into something else. He should phone her up and warn her. He could talk to her. If he couldn't talk to her now . . . Relax. He put his feet back on the table. Cerys was cool. Coolest girl he knew.

Iestyn tried getting to level six on Mega Space Wars but the old skills seemed to have left him. He sat helplessly sinking into the sofa as asteroids the size of small planets crushed his ship.

It was only twelve. He had to do something.

Outside the weather was good and he thought of walking over to Rich's. He didn't want to phone, he felt sort of guilty for not phoning over the last few weeks. He'd just wander over there. Casual.

Rich was in the barn sanding down rust patches on the wheel arches of the Escort.

'Iest! Man, where've you been?'

'Work, you know,' Iestyn shrugged. 'Anyway, I heard you were busy with Martine Lloyd.'

'Not anymore.' Rich sanded furiously. 'Yeah well, you live and learn.'

'Chucked you, did she?'

'I never said that . . .'

'Car's looking good. I thought it was dead.' Iestyn lifted the new red bonnet. 'Engine still mashed?'

Richard stood next to him. The car's insides were still piled together unnaturally. Iestyn looked at the blackened metal and reckoned to himself that if he had been clever he could flog it to Tony for art.

'Yeah. Dad says no new engine until he sees my GCSE results.'

Richard fetched a couple of cans from the farmhouse and they sat in the barn like it was six months ago. Except that Iestyn was dying to say something, just a little something about Cerys. Richard handed Iestyn a tin of white paint to go over the rusty patches and he sprayed obligingly. He did a 'C' first, then covered it over before Rich saw.

'You know that Cerys?'

'Your Rhi's mate? The boffin with legs?'

'Yeah.'

'What about her?'

Iestyn shrugged. 'What d'you reckon?'

Richard looked at him grinning. 'You fancy her? No chance.'

That's all you know, Iestyn said to himself.

'Her and your sister,' Rich shook his head. 'Come on, you know the stories . . .'

Iestyn knew Rhiannon was wild. But she never seemed that wild at home. There was the eyebrow, but everyone on telly or in Rhyl had one and she was really only ever his big sister. There was the time Rhi and Cerys were going to Glastonbury and were lost for ten days. Rhi came back filthy and Iestyn wasn't supposed to be listening but Linda had given her a right going over. Rhi didn't stop grinning for days after that. Iestyn smiled: he knew how she felt now. Maybe Rhi was just having fun. What would she do when Cerys left? What would both of them do?

'What's up with you?'

Iestyn jumped. 'Nothing, nothing. I was just trying to work out how to make a stack at being a fishing warden.'

Richard laughed so much the coke exploded out of his mouth all over the car.

Rhiannon wasn't back when he got home. The house was empty. He still couldn't settle. He walked up the hill behind Cerrig and stopped at the top. All around him the moors stretched away. He gulped in cool air and space, smiled: something was going right.

Iestyn phoned her from the payphone by the War memorial. He'd walked past her house but it was set back from the road and he couldn't see anything. The phone was ringing, he counted six times.

'Hello?' It was her.

'Cerys!' Outside the phone box Jonathan Mottershaw chased Elin and Sophie down the riverbank.

'Iestyn?' she said.

'Yeah. I was wondering, you know, how you were . . .'

Iestyn felt terrified in case she had transformed back into old Cerys.

'Iestyn!' He could see her put her hand up to her mouth, laughing slightly. He could see her mouth.

'After . . . well . . .' *Say* something, Iestyn thought, say something, say you want me to come round now. Say you're coming to pick me up in your car again. Tell me.

'Iestyn . . . I'm fine.' She gave nothing away.

Iestyn swallowed. 'Are you busy . . . sometime, I mean, can I see you?'

'I'll see you tomorrow, at work. You're a good friend, Iestyn. You know that.'

Friend, thought Iestyn, I don't do that with my friends.

'Bye then . . .' He hung up without waiting to hear her say goodbye. He walked, frozen, from the phone box. He wanted too much. He wanted too much. He was so uncool.

69

The lights were on in his house. Rhiannon and Linda had the television on. Linda had a new book, Iestyn didn't see what it was.

'There's some supper in the bottom of the oven, love.'

Iestyn went straight upstairs. He didn't see Rhiannon watching him.

Chapter Eight

Iestyn hadn't slept all night. He'd gone over what he'd say to Cerys and what she'd say back a hundred times. At one point, probably just before dawn, he'd persuaded her to invite him down to London for a long weekend locked in her room. But most of the time she just wouldn't listen. He pictured her air-kissing him goodbye as she got on the train for London.

Iestyn drank half a cup of tea for breakfast and was early for his lift, standing at the junction as Mrs. Hughes's car pulled over. Cerys wasn't there.

'Stomach pains, her mother said.' Mrs. Hughes opened the back door for him.

Iestyn slid into the vinyl seat.

'Iestyn Follett! You don't look so good yourself.' She looked at his reflection in the rear view mirror. 'Must be some virus going round.'

Mr. Barass took one look at Iestyn and sent him home. 'You'll put the fish off with a face like that, let alone the visitors.'

So Iestyn had to sit in the office with Mrs. Hughes until they could find him a lift back down to the village. After an hour and a half listening to the whirr of Mrs. Hughes's PC he went for a walk. 'I need some fresh air, Mrs. H.'

Outside it was beautiful. The reservoir was deep blue and shimmered. Just looking at the jetty stretched out into the water made Iestyn's insides ache. He turned away and walked into the forest.

He walked as far as the main road. If he kept walking, he'd make it home in an hour. It was hot. He could feel the sweat trickling down the side of his head and running behind his ears. He took the waistcoat off and held it scrunched up in his hand. He wished he'd bought some water.

He was sitting down on one of the forestry gates when Tony's van stopped.

'Are you alright? You're looking rough.'

'I've been sent home early. I'm ill.' He looked at Tony and tried a grin on him. 'I'm alright really.'

'Do you want a lift?'

'You're going the wrong way.' Tony was headed north.

'I've just got to fetch some things from the house then I'm going back through the village.'

'You sure?' Iestyn got in.

There was a bottle of lukewarm mineral water that was rolling around on the top of the dashboard. 'Do you mind?' He reached for it and started unscrewing the lid.

'Sure, you have it. It's not exactly cold.'

Iestyn drank it all. Tony wore mirror shades and had some kind of beard growing. Iestyn couldn't find anything to say to him. He was still thinking about Cerys.

'You don't look too happy,' Tony said eventually. 'Trout giving you problems?'

Iestyn didn't reply.

'Fancy a beer?'

'OK.'

Tony headed for The Sportsmans, the highest pub in Wales.

'Listen, they've worked out a date for Fassbinder-Hurley. Seventeenth, they reckon.' He pulled a handful of flyers out of a pocket in his combat trousers. 'Have these, and bring your girlfriend.'

'She's not my girlfriend.'

'Oh. Right. But if that's what your problem is, I reckon you're onto something there.'

'Look, you don't know what you're talking about. OK?' Iestyn was surprised at himself. 'I'm sorry. I'm . . . she's . . . forget it.'

'She's driven as hell, that kid.' Tony shook his head.

'Shame I'm not.'

'No shame in that, mate.'

'I don't mind this place,' Iestyn looked past the car park. 'I really don't. And I have seen a bit, I have seen cities and towns, other places . . .'

'No one has to go anywhere.'

'I know that!' Sometimes this bloke was as dim as his mother. 'I want to stay. But I don't want to be living with me Mam for the rest of my life. I don't want her – Cerys – laughing at me when she comes home for the holidays.'

Tony smiled. 'No, you don't.'

'I don't want to be a fishing warden forever.'

Tony drank his beer and ordered a plate of fried egg and chips.

Iestyn felt his stomach turn over.

'Don't you want anything? Really?'

'Did you always want to be an artist?' Iestyn asked.

Tony shrugged. 'Just happened, I suppose.'

'I don't know what I want.' Iestyn watched two buzzards high up making overlapping circles like Venn diagrams. Tony finished his beer and they drove up to the cottage. Iestyn sat in the van for ages while Tony fetched his bags and a laptop and went round locking doors. 'I have to go back to London. Sort some money out.'

Iestyn closed his eyes and Cerys was breathing into his ear.

I'm in love, he thought. I'm in love and it's already finished.

Chapter Nine

By the time Tony dropped him back in the village it was nearly four. Iestyn realised he'd had nothing to eat since breakfast and bought a couple of rolls in the village shop in case there was no food at home.

He passed Deri in Little George's front garden where they were fixing up their bikes. The back door was open and he pushed his way into the kitchen. He put his rolls down and went upstairs to shower the sweat off.

From his bedroom window he could see his sister lying on a towel in the garden. She was naked apart from her pants. The cordless phone from the kitchen, her bra, and her packet of cigs were in easy reach spread out on the grass. He'd just pulled his sweat-sodden socks off when he heard the phone going off next to her. He watched her reach out with one hand and cover her front with the other as she sat up.

'Cerys!' she said. Iestyn stopped still.

He couldn't catch everything she said. Just the odd things. His name.

His own name. Laughing. Rhi was laughing, sometimes so much she forgot to cover herself and Iestyn saw her tiny pointed tits.

He watched her put her bra on and walk towards the house.

'Don't worry! He'll be OK,' Rhi said. Was Cerys

worried he'd been ill this morning? Rhi laughed again and disappeared into the kitchen.

Iestyn started downstairs quietly. Everything started feeling wrong. Last New Year Bernard Evans at school was selling pills at school. Tiny, tiny pale blue pills. Everyone bought them. For a laugh.

Iestyn thought he'd be dancing all night with a grin a mile wide. But it made him feel like he was walking through custard. Like his limbs were made of lead. It wasn't until they were back at school for the mocks that someone found out they'd all been taking Mrs. Evans's tranquillizers. Iestyn felt the custard feeling thickening round his arms and legs. He moved down the stairs carefully in case he fell. Rhi was in the kitchen talking.

'But I've only got your word that you *actually* did it . . .' she was saying.

'Yeah, I know . . . yeah I *know* . . .' More laughing. Iestyn felt the world was somewhere far away from himself.

'So I owe you now? What are you going to make me do? I did your hair, didn't I? No, not that. Don't make me do that . . . not with Craig Turner!' Hysterical laughter. 'I know! I know. But you said you quite liked Iestyn, said he was sweet . . . You did so! And I can't see me ever even fancying that pig. You said my baby brother was alright! You said! I wouldn't have dared you if he was gross . . .'

Rhiannon stopped. She picked up the white paper bag from the shop with Iestyn's cheese and pickle

76

rolls. On the other side of the kitchen door Iestyn felt a pain between his eyes, a sharp pain for a second then the warm rush as his nose wept blood down his chest.

Rhiannon pushed the door open with her fingertips. They stared at each other. Rhi's tan paled. 'I have to go now. See ya.' She clicked the phone off. Iestyn thought he'd never heard her finish a conversation so fast.

'You need a towel.' She rushed past him to the bathroom.

'It's not much. I'm alright.' He was shaky. He sat down in front of the cheese and pickle rolls. He wasn't hungry. He could feel the blood drying on his face. It had stopped now.

Rhiannon came back. Iestyn looked at her.

'That was me, wasn't it?' he said.

'I got you a towel, you just need to wipe it off. Here.' She dabbed at him with the yellow fluffy towel. Iestyn pulled away.

'That was me, wasn't it? You were talking about me.'

'We were just talking. Look you should get cleaned up. I got you a towel.' She was trying to smile.

'Stop it, Rhi!' Iestyn felt quiet.

'You'll be alright!' She had her babysitting voice on.

'STOP IT, OK?'

Rhiannon backed away. Scared. He hadn't seen his sister scared since Deri tried electrocuting her off her door handle. She'd jumped a foot and gone white as a sheet. She was white as a sheet now.

The phone rang. Rhiannon went to pick it up.

'No. Call me later, alright?' She was half whispering. Iestyn pulled the phone off her.

'It that you? Is it? This is Iestyn. Hello! Hello!' He glared at Rhiannon. 'She put the phone down on me. Not very nice your mate, is she?'

'Iest, it was just . . .' She sighed. 'You're alright, aren't you?' She pulled the loops out of the towel with her fingers. 'You're alright, you were great yesterday weren't you, just after, you know.' She tried smiling but Iestyn could see she was still scared.

'Yeah. Me, I'm just fine.' He got up watching her flinch as he pushed the table away in front of him. 'Tell your mate. Next time . . .'

Linda Follett kicked the back door open with her foot. She had her overall on, a book in one hand and a plastic bag full of individual mayonnaise and ketchup sachets in the other.

'Don't say hello then, it's only your mother . . .'

Iestyn banged upstairs.

'What's up with him?'

Iestyn shut his bedroom door and put a tape on. He turned the volume up so that he didn't think. It didn't work. It was the tape from Tony, old soppy reggae stuff that knotted up in his chest.

It had been a dare. She'd done it for a dare. She was eighteen, it wasn't possible . . . his sister! Cerys never even liked him. Never even liked him. What

78

did she get? A hairdo and what else what was he worth? A tenner? Rhi's favourite nail varnish?

Rhiannon was knocking on his door. Iestyn was sat against the other side, saying nothing. He stretched his hand out to the tape player and turned up the tape. He wanted it loud enough to fill up his head. But he could still hear his sister banging, kicking it felt like.

'Iestyn, listen! Please!'

What an idiot. He couldn't believe how stupid, how bloody stupid he had been. She didn't even *like* him. Never had liked him, never had fancied him. Rhiannon stopped banging.

Why did he even think she'd ever liked him? She was a low-life, lying slut. He banged his fist down onto the floor, felt his knuckles graze on the thin nylon carpet. He felt his bones jar and his skin buzz. That felt better than the numbness before. He stood up and banged his fist into the wall. Again and again and again until there was first a dent and then a sizeable hole in the plaster board wall.

Rhiannon pushed through into the room and stared at him. She looked different. Iestyn thought of hitting her in case she started laughing at him. He wanted to hit her. Hit them. Smash their faces into pulp. He was going mad. He had to get out of here before he knocked the place down.

Iestyn barged out of the house leaving the door banging open behind him. He could hear Linda calling after him too, but he kept walking. His skin buzzed from his fingertips to his knuckles where the skin was broken and bloody, up his arms into his head. He pushed through the front gate walking in big wide strides, hands clenched in tight fists.

He kept walking. He heard Rhiannon shouting after him, yelling sorry, but he kept walking. He kept walking until he was outside Cerys's house.

The vicarage had a big drive and high hedges. He kept walking, making the loose gravel crunch under his trainers. He almost stopped. Just before he rounded the side of the house to the kitchen door Iestyn paused: he could hear a radio – that had to be her – and he kept walking.

Cerys was lying on a white plastic sunbed reading the *Time Out Student Guide to London*. She was wearing a washed-out blue bikini top and shorts. She didn't hear him.

The garden was normal. Everything around him was normal. Just the pressure building up behind his eyes, in his fists and the buzzing all over. Only that wasn't normal.

She turned round, hand to her chest, 'Oh, my God, Iestyn! You made me jump!'

Iestyn didn't say anything. Behind her sunglasses Cerys's eyes flicked from his strained face to his bloody fists. Iestyn saw her pulse jump under the skin in her throat. She's scared, he thought. Good.

'Iestyn!' Her face was blanching, even in the sun.

He thought he was going to cry. He didn't want to scare her, he wanted to kiss her. She put the book down spine up, squashing it open.

'Iestyn, look.'

It's always 'look' when it's lies, Iestyn thought.

She swung her legs off the sunbed and pulled her shades off. 'I'm sorry.' She bit her lip. 'You know. It wasn't supposed to . . . supposed to get like this. I really like you.'

Iestyn couldn't say anything, he just stared at her. How could she like him? It was a joke. She wasn't upset inside at all. She tugged at her bikini.

'I didn't mean to upset you like this, I thought you'd, well . . .' She shrugged. 'I thought it would be . . . fun,' She smiled lamely, scrabbling with her feet for the flip flops under the lounger. A couple of swallows chased each other, flying low over the lawn.

Iestyn felt the anger rising up all over him, making the buzzing harder in his sore hands. He kicked at the barbecue set by the garage and sent it spinning across the grass. The noise stopped him feeling. But only for a second.

'Iestyn!' She sounded just like his big sister.

'What was I worth? Tell me . . . What did you get for doing it with me? That hair? A tenner? A fiver? Just a good laugh?'

She started crying. 'That's not fair, Iestyn! You know it wasn't like that!'

'I don't know anything, me.'

'Iestyn. My parents will be back soon. I think you should go.' She wiped her eyes. Sniffed.

'I'm not going yet. Tell me, tell me what am I worth?'

He felt the tingling up his arms and into his chest. 'TELL ME!'

Cerys was quivering now, as if it was his fault. He stared hard at her standing by the sunbed, quaking, then he picked up one of the matching patio chairs and threw it at the French windows. He heard the noise of the glass crackling and felt the breaking all over his skin, through his teeth, everywhere. He looked at her looking at him. She didn't see that he was breaking. She didn't see that at all. She just saw a nutter. Iestyn ran back down the path before he came apart completely.

Chapter Ten

The Laughing Chef was nearly empty. One fat trucker with hairy arms was in the far corner reading the *Liverpool Echo* propped up against the squeezy ketchup. He was eating the all-day-breakfast and he had two mugs of tea. Iestyn recognised him as Seventh Day Dave, one of Mum's regulars. Mum was standing at the griddle.

'Iest, love?' Just him being here meant something was up. 'Everything alright? Deri? Rhi?'

'Yeah, Ma, they're fine.'

Linda Follett flicked some button mushrooms over and pushed them together again, rounding them up like little grey sheep with her see-through spatula.

'Are you hungry, love?'

Iestyn shrugged. He didn't know. He did feel something, it might be hunger. He pushed his grazed hands into the pockets of his jeans so she wouldn't see them.

Linda smiled. 'I'll do you a fry up, love.'

She cracked the egg and peeled two pinky strips of bacon out of their plastic down onto the griddle.

'You sit down.' Iestyn sat with his back to the trucker, his face to the window looking out across the moor. It rose up towards the horizon in strips of green and orange, edge to edge beyond the plate glass.

Linda bought him the plate of food and sat down

opposite, mouthing something to Alwen behind the counter.

Iestyn squeezed the bottle of ketchup onto the middle of the egg then pierced the yellow yolk with his fork and swirled it until it was orange. Force of habit, Iestyn thought. He looked down at the now fluorescent egg and the pink fleshy bacon. The grilled tomato looked like a wound and the mushrooms glistened with fat. He thought of the word 'suppurating' from when they'd been doing the War poets at school and he had to put his fork down. He couldn't eat any of it.

Outside the cars swished through Cerrig. He thought of Cerys getting up and buttoning her polyester blouse ready for work, running her hand through her hair, brushing her eyelashes with dark mascara like he'd seen Rhi do.

Iestyn pushed the red and white plate away.

'I can't work there any more, Mam. I just can't.'

He never meant to say it like that; overdramatic, melodramatic. The fork was still stuck into the heart of the leaking egg.

'I can't.' That was calmer. He lifted his eyes to hers. She wasn't there. As usual. That was the problem. Linda was off in some book, out on the moor in an off-the-shoulder number being pursued by a swarthy trucker in a frock coat.

Seventh Day Dave burped and wiped his lips with one hairy arm. Iestyn shook his head.

'Never mind.'

'You not eating, love?'

'I don't think I'm hungry, Ma. I'm just tired.'

Linda's green eyes caught the light.

'I've got to go, Ma,' he said.

'But you've not finished,'

'No, I mean I've got to get away.' He breathed deep. He didn't want to upset her. 'I'm going to visit Dad. I phoned him up.'

'Neil? Are you sure that's what you want?'

Iestyn nodded.

'But what about your job?'

Iestyn pushed his seat back and stood up. 'That's what I said, Ma.' He sighed. 'I just can't do it any more.'

Linda picked up the plate. She looked sad. 'Do you think I want to be doing this?' she said.

Iestyn had already pushed open the heavy glass door and left.

Rhiannon was out of the house when he got back, keeping out of his way. Deri was sprawled on the sofa playing Mega Space Wars with Little George from next door.

The bedroom was a mess. Iestyn found the big black sportsbag and started stuffing it with clean underwear. At the end of his bed he found the shirt he'd been wearing. That was only two days ago.

It seemed unbelievable that he had ever been so happy. Iestyn sniffed it, held it, then threw it into the black hole under Deri's bed. Downstairs they had only got as far as Level 3.

'I'm going then.' Iestyn stood in the doorway. The two boys said nothing. 'I'm off.'

'Bye, Iestyn.' Little George was at least polite.

'Are you coming back for the Comet, then?' Deri pressed Pause and pushed his specs up his nose.

'Dunno.' That was only three weeks away. He planned on staying away longer than that.

'Can I have the CD player?' Deri asked. Iestyn glared and Deri added, ''Til you get back?'

''Til I get back.'

Deri pressed continue and the TV was a mass of meteorites and alien spacecraft. Iestyn thought about telling them that they couldn't beat the mothership without full laser shield. But he didn't.

He shut the front door. The village was quiet and normal. He planned to get a lift or a bus to Wrexham and pick up the train from there.

Iestyn walked down to the main road, swung his bag down to the ground and stuck his thumb out. A sheep lorry, a Kelpie tourer camper van, and Mrs. Roberts from the mobile library passed, but no one stopped. In the end the bus came and he pictured Cerys up at the reservoir laughing with Rhiannon. Just in case he had any second thoughts.

The train took ages to come. He sat on the platform until it rolled in.

It was a tinny, rattly thing full of not-quite-students on their way back east from summer courses at the university at Aber. They all had wah-wah voices and looked like they hadn't slept for a week. Nearly all the girls reminded him of Cerys. One, in the farthest corner, had a mouth the same colour as Cerys's. When she spoke it made the same shapes on her face.

It made him ache. The girl was laughing. She had no idea.

He could see Cerys coming back from university with three London boyfriends who all drove powder blue Jaguars and had wallets full of gold cards. That was what she wanted. Clubs and money and men. Not hick schoolboys doing NVQs in trout recognition. He was suddenly so sad he could hardly move.

As the train shambled east the buildings spread and grew. Iestyn sat tight, not looking at the Cerys-girl and trying to remember where Dad's house was in relation to the station. He was at Telford by early evening. He bought a Mars bar and a Coke outside the station and tried to read the map inside his head. Everything looked different. There were roundabouts with no pavements and underpasses tiled pale grey. Pedestrian bridges over roads looked like they'd blow over in the wind. There were spiral space age ramps instead of steps, and sky-blue roadsigns pointing to motorways.

Iestyn climbed a ramp and looked down at the town spread out in a soft valley around a spine of motorway. Somewhere, in one of those brown tiled houses on a crescent or a close – a close like Brookside, he thought – was Dad's house. He stood watching the traffic for a moment, more than enough traffic for a shedful of Laughing Chefs. The cars flashed by, silver like water down the side of the hill at the back of Cerrig. Flowing. If he faced the sun and narrowed his eyes the cars all squeezed into a continuous metal blur.

He found the house before dark. It was a small close shaped like a frying pan with houses staring at each other across a patch of green and tarmac. There were several small children pushing plastic tractors along with the tips of their toes. A couple of older ones, on bikes, looked like kids at home, but cleaner, thought Iestyn. Some his age sat round an open garage door passing cigarettes hidden in their hands. Iestyn rang the bell. The door was glass, swirly patterned, so he could make out a figure on the other side. But it was wobbly and distorted as if it had been beamed down from Io and scrambled on the way. He thought of Deri and looked for any signs of the comet in the darkening sky. The lights were coming on in the close, brighter than stars.

Natalie, Neil's wife, opened the door. She was wearing her building society uniform of royal blue skirt and white blouse with little darts of optimistic colour. She smoothed her hair and took off her gold ear-rings and looked down the hall for Neil.

'Neil! Neil! Iestyn's here!'

'Sssh!' Neil appeared out of the farthest door, closing it slowly behind him. 'I've only just got Courtney Rose off to sleep.' He smiled at Iestyn. 'She's teething.'

Chapter Eleven

The air tasted different in Telford. He noticed as soon as he woke, which was five-fifteen by the giant digital clock balanced on the bedside table next to his fold-out bed. Courtney Rose *was* teething: he could hear her through the paper-thin walls, sucking in the air and wailing it out. He listened for a good five minutes, then rolled off the bed and up out of the room.

The baby was standing up in her cot, mouth open wailing, eyes like slits. Iestyn could see the wet patch on her babygro across her tummy. He bent down and picked her up. Rhiannon used to babysit for the Lloyd twins Thursday nights and he had taken it over when she was busy. The Lloyd twins had a little sister too, Catrin. She'd been bigger than Courtney Rose but he could still remember how to do a nappy.

At breakfast, Neil was ecstatic. 'You changed her! Bloody brilliant!'

Natalie was less impressed but she was off to work without even registering him. Neil said on Mondays there was a really good parent and toddler session in the community hall and why didn't he take Courtney when they obviously got on so well? Neil said it would be a great help, because then he could get the shopping in and drop in on his mate Trev who had said last week that he might have a little bit of driving and, well, you never know.

The door had slammed before he had time to say anything.

This wasn't what he had imagined. Still, he picked up Courtney Rose's changing bag which matched the three-in-one buggy he strapped her into and set off. He could see Rich laughing at him. At least there weren't many people about. No kids hanging around.

Courtney Rose was out of the buggy and all over the sticky rubber matting put down specially for the Parent and Toddler morning. The other mothers smiled gooey mothery smiles at him and chatted in corners and he felt as useless as a maggot in a fly fishing lake.

He realised Courtney Rose was attacking some runny-faced boy by crumbling a jaffa cake over his head. Iestyn went and pulled her off and wiped most of the jaffa cake out of the boy's hair. The boy was with a girl, not a woman – a big sister or aunty, Iestyn thought. She didn't look more than fifteen, sixteen. She had a vague smooth face, nice teeth though, and hair tied in a plait that snaked down her back. Iestyn was just thinking how much sexier Cerys was when he shut that idea out and walked over to her. Maybe this girl could make him think about something else.

'Sorry about that,' Iestyn said.

'Forget it.' The girl was wiping jaffa cake off her fingers with a baby wipe. She smiled at him. She was wearing two gold chains; one said 'Lorraine' in fat swooping letters, the other said 'No. 1 Mum'.

She saw him looking and rubbed at the letters with her fingers.

'Yeah, he's mine.'

'Lovely.' Iestyn knew he sounded dumb. 'He's, um, lovely.'

'Wish his Dad thought so,' Lorraine said. 'Is she not yours then?' She pointed over to where Courtney Rose was demolishing some Lego.

'No, half-sister.'

Sitting close, Iestyn could see the dark under her eyes where she hadn't slept.

'Is he teething then?'

'Yeah,' she said. She smiled at him but Iestyn could feel something close to desperation off her.

'I think my little sister's had just about enough now,' Iestyn said, and he finished his free cup of tea and ate his biscuit and strapped Courtney Rose back into her buggy. She fell asleep before they were anywhere near home. Iestyn thought he'd try the shops, maybe there was a job centre. After all, he had to start looking for something else now.

The job centre was useless. Nothing he could do. Security Guards, he could do that, but not pay rent or afford to eat or anything like that. And he got the feeling that Natalie was not over the moon about him staying indefinitely.

They all wanted qualifications and experience, and although it was only another week until his results came through, the only experience he had was as a fishing warden.

Outside the job centre the traffic rolled on. Not much call for fishing wardens round here.

Chapter Twelve

Cerys wrote him a letter after he'd been gone four days.

He was in the kitchen drinking coffee when he heard the post. A quick metallic click-click as the letterbox flapped open then shut. The kitchen clock said six-thirty. Courtney Rose was asleep in his lap dribbling like Jabba the Hutt in a babygro. No one else was up. Last night Linda had phoned. She tried to persuade him to come home. She'd talked to Mr. Barass who'd said he'd hold the job for him for a week. These things happen, she said. What things happen? he thought. What had Rhi told him?

He told Linda he wasn't coming back. Said he might be going to Spain with Neil and Natalie. That was a lie, because they'd booked their tickets. But Iestyn didn't want to go back at least until October when he could be sure that all traces of Cerys would have gone.

He could hear Rhi breathing on the kitchen phone listening.

'Ask her – go on, Mam, ask her what happened.' And he hung up. She phoned again and talked to Neil. Iestyn didn't bother listening.

The coffee was cold so he made some more, moving slowly around the kitchen balancing the comatose Courtney Rose on his shoulder.

It was another five minutes before anyone else was up.

Natalie came down and had a go at him for drinking hot coffee with Courtney Rose lying there.

'You could scald her, burn her!' Natalie yelled and Courtney Rose's mouth opened slowly into a scream. Iestyn said nothing and passed her over and walked upstairs. The letter was on the hall mat. He knew it was from her. His heart jumped and fell. He picked it up scrunching it in his hand and running upstairs two at a time. The stamp had a dragon in the corner and her writing was small and spiky. She'd just written his first name in capitals like she was shouting at him. He closed his eyes: IESTYN, she said. She looked terrified. She was wearing the blue bikini top. He wanted to tear the letter up. He knew what it would say; that he was sweet, that he was good. That she was wrong and bad and most of all that she was sorry.

He looked at his name on the envelope and smoothed out the wrinkles.

IESTYN. He turned the dirty white envelope over and picked off the sticky tape. Slowly he opened it. It was white plain paper. One line, capitals again – shouting. He read it once quickly without taking it in in case it hurt too much: I'M NOT SORRY. Cerys xxxxx.

Five kisses. Kisses on the cheek like when he'd got out of the car. Those sort of throwaway skin-grazing kisses that mean nothing.

He read the words again. I'M NOT SORRY. He wasn't crying, it was just his face smarting. He should be glad. She wasn't sorry. He couldn't sit still. She wasn't sorry? She wasn't sorry for what? For what happened, for hurting him, for what? It had only made things worse. He wished she were dead and he couldn't feel. He stayed in his room and watched Natalie squeeze into her shiny green Vauxhall Corsa, then waited while Dad got Courtney Rose ready and trundled her out of the close.

He thought about phoning Cerys but it would end up like their last conversations, him shouting at her or worse, both of them saying nothing. He thought about writing back and spent the morning tearing pages out of Natalie's Basildon Bond writing pad. Iestyn couldn't come up with one-liners like Cerys. He had too much to say. He was still in love with her. He knew technically he couldn't be; she hadn't even fancied him, had only gone along with any of it because Rhiannon had dared her. But that's what it felt like. Why wasn't she sorry? He addressed the envelope first. Lower case. cerys ap iwan. Rifled through a letter rack and a drawer in the kitchen for a stamp. Stuck it on. Then he tore out the last page of paper. He wrote: WHY NOT? and sent it quickly before he could change his mind.

Chapter Thirteen

Linda forwarded his GCSE results and they arrived the same day as Cerys's reply. Rhiannon had written an apology too. He threw it away. He didn't want to talk to his sister. Natalie made him a cup of coffee and looked interested. Iestyn couldn't figure out why. Did she want to gloat when he got seven unclassifieds? He took all his post upstairs. The envelopes lay on the spare bed and he looked from one to the other before deciding which one to open first: GCSEs. Cerys. Cerys. GCSEs.

He opened the exams first. Iestyn read the sliver of paper three times. Six Bs and a D. And the D was only History. For a second he thought about going back to school, waving his bit of paper right in all those teachers' faces. It didn't last. They'd probably think he was coached by Deri. Still, Linda was going to be well pleased.

He almost ran down to the phone to tell her. Then he remembered.

Cerys's letter. He tore open the envelope. He could see through the paper – more than one line of writing this time. He turned it over.

Iestyn, she said, if you promise not to break anything (Iestyn's insides turned over,) talk to me. I'm leaving at the end of September. Are you coming back? I'm not sorry because that night was lovely. Not fake.

NOT FAKE. I can't do this with letters.

Cerys. xxxxx

'How do I know you're not fake?' Iestyn said out loud.

Downstairs, Natalie and Neil were waiting.

'Bad as all that, Iestyn?' Natalie poured him some coffee.

'I'm sure you did your best,' Neil said.

Iestyn sipped his coffee and looked at Natalie sitting there smug.

'That's the mad thing. You know, I didn't. Do my best.'

Natalie smiled.

'Look.' Iestyn passed the piece of paper over.

'Bloody hell, lad!' Neil slapped him on the back. 'Nat, look at this!

'Well done!'

'No As.' Natalie stopped smiling. 'Still, you can do a lot with grades like these. They're always looking for juniors at work.'

'And there's college or A levels.' Neil was as happy as if he'd done the exams himself. 'You'd better phone your mother. Put her out of her misery.'

Linda was thrilled. She wanted him home, it was her last week at work and she'd saved him a Tennessee Swamp Mud Tart, the chocolate one, his favourite. Iestyn was quiet.

'Rhiannon's leaving,' Linda said.

'So?'

'She's got a job in a tattooist's in Manchester.'

'Oh.'

'Iestyn, love! Can't you two talk to each other? It's

96

driving me up the wall. I do not need this right now.'
She sighed. 'Please? Before she goes. Come home,
love. Before I go mad. I don't know what's wrong
with this family, I really don't.'

Iestyn said nothing. His family was not his
responsibility.

'Iestyn?'

'Hmm?'

'Your results. Best news all year. Really.'

'Thanks, Mam.'

Iestyn went out for a drink with Neil.

'You deserve it,' Neil said.

Iestyn worried for a moment about Courtney Rose
left alone with Natalie, a woman whose shiny fingernails seemed to prevent intimate human contact,
especially with babies. But she hurried them out of
the house.

'I'm sure you two have got a lot to talk about.' She
said this slowly at, rather than to, Neil. 'And anyway,
Jen's coming round with her Avon stuff. I don't want
you lot hanging around.'

Neil took him to a pub by a canal. The traffic noise
was there, filtered through new trees. Tall slim
speckled birches, they didn't smell like pines. Iestyn
let Neil buy him a half, but he couldn't think what to
say. When Neil asked him what he wanted to do with
his life he didn't know. He shrugged, looked down at
the flat murky canal water. You could see clear to the
pebbles at the reservoir.

'No fish in there!' Then he thought of the job he'd

jacked in and wished he hadn't. He'd only been here ten days and he wanted to go home.

He wanted to go round to Rich's, see how he'd done. See if his old man would let them have the quads out again. Iestyn looked at his Dad. He was trying to say something. Iestyn stopped thinking about home and drank his beer.

'Natalie's alright, you know.' Neil said it like he was apologising.

'I never said nothing.'

'You don't need to! She's different to your mother. To Linda.'

'You're telling me!'

'Linda almost ruined everything. But I let her.'

'What do you mean?' Iestyn sat up. 'Why did you leave?'

'I had to. We had this happy family set up. Poor but happy, I thought. I thought she was. You know Linda. Always looking somewhere else.

'When I met her, she said, "Let's go to Wales, space for the kids". Rhiannon wasn't even born then. "We'll have a cottage", she said. A garden she wanted.

'And where do we fetch up? Bloody Cerrig! Where nothing grows more than three feet tall and the scenery's crap!' Neil laughed.

Iestyn felt homesick.

'She always wanted something else. When she went off with that bloke, that man, Merlin-Mervyn . . .'

'Myrddin ap Nefydd.'

'That's it! I felt, I felt . . .' He paused. Iestyn looked at the grey hair at the side of Neil's head. 'I felt gutted. All I had, all I had was just taken away. Was just fake. She was fake. Putting the dinner on the table and then going out with him! I had to go. Couldn't stay. It was for the best. Natalie's a good woman. I've got everything now.' He drained his glass. 'Even a son who does bloody brilliant in his exams!'

Iestyn knew what was coming. He listened as Neil urged him to get a job like Natalie's – 'Can't beat security, lad!' – and as Neil told him how much his mother missed him. How he and Natalie would rather he didn't come to Spain. How the house was getting full. How Natalie needed her space. How Linda needed all the help she could get.

When they got back, Courtney Rose was fast asleep and Natalie had a friend round demonstrating a colour corrective foundation and moisturising complex.

'See, goes on so lightly you don't know it's there!' the friend gushed, 'and if you go all blotchy, like me, it just covers it up. There!'

She held up a hand mirror for Natalie. 'Beautiful!'

Chapter Fourteen

Iestyn packed the next day. He hadn't even stuck it two weeks.

Neil and Courtney Rose came to see him off at the station and waved at him as the train for Wrexham pulled out. He put his bag on the seat next to him and shut his eyes. He'd have to go to Mr. Barass and beg for his job back. He'd have to forget Cerys existed.

At Wrexham he hitched as far as Llangollen, got a lift off an Insectocutor salesman:

'We make the blue light flykillers . . . best if you've a problem with flying insects . . .'

The man was as driven as Cerys. Iestyn was glad to get out of the car. It was Sunday, so there weren't any buses. He was thinking about walking when a powder-blue Jaguar stopped beside him.

'Hi!' Connie opened the door. 'Need a lift?'

The seats were ivory leather and the dashboard was shiny pale knotted wood.

'This is beautiful!'

'I know. I always wanted one, right from school.' Connie shifted gear. 'It's fast, too.' She grinned and stepped hard on the accelerator.

Iestyn enjoyed the ride. Seventy, eighty round all the bends as the road climbed towards the moors. Better than a jeep.

'Have you seen Tone lately?' Connie asked. 'He's

not too down? He always gets so edgy before something like this.'

'I've been away.'

'Tony's got Carl and a couple of riggers coming to help out. You've not seen them around? Are they all up at the house?

Iestyn shook his head. 'I don't know.'

'Oh, well, I'll have to find out for myself.' The car slowed towards the village. 'Shall I drop you here?' Connie pulled up by the war memorial. 'I nearly forgot!' She killed the engine and took a box from the back seat. 'Photos, look. You and your girlfriend.'

Iestyn looked. Colour photos, black around the edges where it was night, the red glowing of the fire and his face and Cerys's face *that* close. That close. There were two pictures, almost identical, shiny paper that slid in his hand.

'Aah,' Connie said starting the engine, 'young love!' and the Jaguar pulled away.

Iestyn couldn't bring himself to throw them away. He walked, numb, towards the row of council houses and pushed open the kitchen door. Mum was at work. Deri was still on the computer with Little George.

It was like he'd never gone away.

Upstairs he could hear Rhiannon in her bedroom moving around.

Iestyn went up and put his stuff down and sat on his bed. His fishing warden clothes lay on the floor, the waistcoat in a pile between Alpha Centuri and Sirius. The hole in the plasterboard wall had wept white dust onto the Milky Way. He shut the photos and Cerys's letter in his desk drawer.

When he looked up Rhiannon was standing in the doorway. She knocked on the open door.

'Can I come in?'

Iestyn shrugged.

'How's Dad, then? Courtney Whatsit?'

'Fine. They're fine.'

'Are you . . . alright?'

'Mam said you had a job. In Manchester.'

'Yeah. I'm going next week. You can have my bedroom if you like.'

She sat down on Deri's bed on the other side of the room. She was wearing Deri's old Spiderman pyjama top as a T-shirt.

'I have to say sorry. We shouldn't have . . . well it wasn't just my idea. She said, Cerys said, after that first day at the lake . . .'

'Reservoir,' Iestyn said.

'Reservoir then, she said she fancied you.'

'Look, Rhi, I don't want any of this. Alright? Don't try telling me it was all real, don't try telling me anything . . .' Iestyn shut his eyes and lay back on his bed.

'Iestyn, you've got to believe me!'

'Believe what? Forget it, Rhi! I just want to forget it.'

'Sure?'

'Sure.'

The relief on Rhiannon's face was obvious.

'Leave me alone. Alright?'

'Sure.'

She left. Iestyn shut the door and took the photos and the letter out. That was the problem, he thought. He didn't want to forget. Maybe he should burn them.

Linda came back from work late after a goodbye drink with the girls. She smelt of gin and fried bread and almost fell over in the kitchen.

'Iestyn! It's so good to have you home!' She kissed him, aiming for his face but nuzzling into his shoulder. Iestyn didn't want his Mam like this. For a second he thought of Natalie, in her suits with her eyebrows plucked and re-directed. Linda must have seen it.

She slumped into one of the kitchen chairs, looking sad and looking at him.

'You know, Iest. It doesn't get any different when you're grown up. You do stupid things and you do them again and again. It's living.'

Linda hadn't taken the chocolate cake out of the freezer so they ate it rock hard, cutting it with the electric bread knife Deri won in a school raffle. Rhiannon said she couldn't eat it and went out and Deri went to bed so Iestyn sat with Linda and helped her upstairs. He allowed himself one look at the photos before he went to sleep.

Monday morning, Mr. Barass was adamant. The job would go to someone else. There were plenty of young men, and women for that matter, with the determination and commitment – he stressed *commitment* – who would snap up the chance of a position at North Wales's premier trout-fishing venue. Iestyn said he was sorry, but it was no good. Arwel Hughes, son of Mrs. Hughes, would be filling in until he went back to university.

What was he going to tell Linda? Iestyn reckoned she was still hung over and wouldn't surface for hours. Iestyn thought he'd take her some tea. Break it to her gently.

'Iestyn, making your old mother a cup of tea! What have I done to deserve this?' Linda was up, dressed and made-up. Not quite the full Natalie, Iestyn thought.

'Where are you going, Ma?' He put the tea down in front of her.

'Is it that obvious? I'm enrolling at college. A levels. English and History. I always fancied that. Yvonne – Mrs. Roberts – told me I'd be mad not to! I'm starting at the end of the month. If they'll take me.'

Iestyn sat down. Deri would put it down to the comet. Millennial stress. His mother going to college and Rhiannon getting a job. Maybe they'd be moving to a house with a garage and two toilets.

'Are you sure that's right, Ma? I mean, college is for me or Rhi, you're supposed to go to work, earn money. The place'll be full of kids my age, from my school. Are you sure you're not too old?'

'Iestyn!' She was laughing. 'What do you expect

me to do? Sit on my backside all day? I've got to do something or I'll go up the wall.'

Iestyn thought of himself stuck at home in an empty house, with Deri at school, Linda at college sat at the desk next to Rich, and Rhiannon making holes in ravers in Manchester.

'Don't worry, we'll be alright. It's not as if we ever had any money in the first place.'

'It's not the money, Ma. I haven't got a job anymore.'

'Ah,' said Linda.

She made them both croissants. 'So you'll be off away, like Rhi. Not exactly heaving with jobs round here, are we?' She sipped her tea carefully so her lipstick didn't come off on the mug. 'You could always come to college with your old Ma!' She looked at him. 'Maybe not.'

Iestyn looked out of the window. All he could see was the grey wall of next door's where someone had scratched 'She smells' into the pebble dash. But he knew that beyond were the moors and the space and the open sky that Linda had brought them here for.

'I'm not going away, Ma. I'll find something.'

Chapter Fifteen

'They've got it wrong, they've got it all wrong!' Deri ran into the house 'It's coming at the end of the week. This week!'

Iestyn was still stuck in the asteroid belt. He'd been there for most of the week he'd been home, curtains drawn, TV on. Richard was busy with the farm and Martine Lloyd again. He phoned to say he'd passed his test and Martine couldn't resist a man with a Land Rover. Cerys had phoned once. Iestyn wouldn't talk to her. It felt easier like that, he didn't want to end up hitting something.

Deri stood in front of the TV and clicked it off. 'See, Iest!'

He was waving one of Anthony Cullinan's flyers. 'They've got it all wrong.'

'Deri! You idiot! I haven't saved!'

'Forget it, Iest, you've been stuck there for ages now! Even me and George are at the Death Planet!'

'Deri, just leave me alone. Alright?'

'But Iest, you know this bloke,' He waved the flyer. 'You can tell him, he's got to re-schedule!' Deris tugged the curtains open and the light was strong and yellow.

'What time is it, Der?'

'Half-three. Look, Iest, I want you to tell him!'

Deri wouldn't stop until Iestyn found Tony's business card in his fishing waistcoat.

'You phone him: you know him!'

Iestyn dialled. 'His mobile's switched off, Deri – listen!'

'Try again!'

Tony picked it up.

'Iestyn Follett! How's the nose?' Iestyn could hear banging in the background.

'Fine, fine.'

'Sorry about the noise, we've started building by the reservoir, full size this time. Where've you been? You should come and look!'

'Iest! Tell him about the comet!'

Iestyn tried. In the end Deri wrenched the phone from his brother and went on and on and on about solar flares, winds in space and the possibility of collision with earth.

Iestyn got bored of waiting to have the phone back and flicked the game back on.

'He's cool,' Deri said at least twenty minutes later. 'He's got a mate in this observatory in the Canary Islands. They've been tracking it, and he's already changed the date.'

Iestyn's ship got hit by an asteroid.

'He says you're to bring me up to the site, where he's making the sculpture things. He's got *actual* faxes from the observatory with Fassbinder Hurley's trajectory!'

Iestyn's ship exploded. Deri shook his head.

'You can't do that bit without full laser shield, Iest!'

Iestyn hadn't been up at the reservoir for weeks. He got the bus with Deri and walked down through the car park and passed the visitors' centre to the water. A few metres down the waterside he could see Tony's van and some wooden scaffolding that looked a bit like a half-size adventure playground.

'Iest, can we not get a can? I'm that thirsty.'

'You get on. I'm staying here.' He didn't want to go inside.

Iestyn walked across to the jetty and sat down. He just had to let Cerys go. She was going to London and she didn't care and that was reality. Inside his head it was pitch dark and he was moving through the black water with Cerys. What he needed, apart from a selective lobotomy, was a job. He looked around at the lake and the boats. The water board jeep wasn't parked up, so Mr. Barass was probably off somewhere scaring schoolkids with no licences. The office was open. He pushed the door and went in.

Inside, Mr. Barass was restocking flies.

'Mr. Barass! I thought you were out . . . the jeep.'

Mr. Barass smiled. He'd shaved off his moustache and Iestyn could see that he wasn't really that old, not like his mother or Mrs. Hughes.

The jeep was just up at the marina. Mr. Barass didn't say anything about Iestyn's replacement.

'How's Arwel getting on? ' Iestyn asked, 'Only if anything does come up, I'd still be . . . you know . . . interested . . .'

Mr. Barass said nothing, but carried on sorting the tiny feathered flies into different boxes. Iestyn wished he'd never said anything. Outside he could see Deri looking for him, can in hand.

'I just want you to know, Mr. Barass, it'd never happen again.'

Mr. Barass smiled. He put the flies away and went into the back office, coming back with an envelope.

'Read this, lad.'

It had a stamp and his name and address.

'It were due for posting today.'

Iestyn opened the letter. It was addressed to Mr. Follett.

Arwel Hughes was going back to Sheffield in October, the letter said. Due to Iestyn's previous work record, if he would like to be considered for his old job, he could have it back in October under a new probationary contract.

'That means if you blow it this time you're out for good!' Mr. Barass said, smiling though.

Six months probation from October. He could do it.

'I won't blow it, Mr. Barass. Thanks a lot. You will not regret this!'

Iestyn ran out of the office straight into Deri.

'I got my job back, Der, I got my job! There is some justice!'

There was no shade and Iestyn was running with sweat by the time they made it to the site.

Tony was piling cut wood into the heart of the

spiral sculpture. This one was at least three times as big as the one Iestyn had seen in the orchard.

There were also three smaller structures placed around the large spiral. 'You see, Iest,' Tony said, 'these smaller ones go up first, and they're doused with solvent to make them burn blue.'

Deri was impressed. 'You set fire to this stuff?'

Tony nodded.

'Cool!'

'You want the faxes? They're in the van.'

Deri and Tony poured over the coils of faxes. Iestyn walked round the site. There was a man digging a trench round the big sculpture and a woman wheeling barrowloads of wood from a trailer.

Deri was ages. He persuaded Tony to give them a lift home and asked him in. Deri showed him his map of the stars and then introduced him to Linda who was embarrassingly nice.

'Have a cup of tea, Anthony, coffee maybe?'

Iestyn went out. He walked round the village, and thought about going over to Rich's. But he found himself outside Cerys's.

He looked into the drive. Her parents' cars were both parked up; there was no point trying to talk to her. He had to let her go.

Chapter Sixteen

On the night of the comet, Iestyn went up early with Deri. Iestyn was too busy to notice anything at first, then he realised the field beyond the site was filling up with people and stalls. The car park was full. People had come from miles away.

'What do you expect?' Deri said. 'Doesn't happen every day. And it's going to look brilliant, see. The clouds are going.'

Iestyn looked up and the sky was massive. The high, flat moors stretched west to where the sun was setting red behind the mountains. The lakeside hummed with clouds of midges. All the telescopes pointed north west.

'That's where it's coming from,' Deri pointed, then traced an arc across the sky. 'You get it?'

Iestyn nodded. He'd never seen a comet before. Only pictures of flaming fireballs in books.

'This is going to be the best night of my life!' Deri said, and believed it, you could tell.

'Grow up, Der,' Iestyn said, but Deri had already run off.

Iestyn scanned the crowd and suddenly saw Cerys, standing by the barrier talking to Connie. She had her arms folded, and her skirt was blowing against her body in the breeze. He looked away then walked away, in case she saw him.

Tony was worried about the wind. 'It's going to

blow the fire sideways!' Deri jumped about with Little George telling people where they should stand. Deri had brought his telescope and set it up just beyond the car park. There was a mini forest of telescopes and a whole army of comet-watchers. Iestyn counted five 'Eyes on the Skies' T-shirts, and six with 'The Truth is out There.' There were stalls selling inflatable aliens and a bloke sitting cross-legged under a pyramid-shaped frame meditating.

Iestyn sat on the jetty. Watching.

'Hello.' Cerys came and sat next to him. He almost got up and walked off. He looked into the water. In the fading light it was almost completely black. Like that other time, he thought.

Iestyn didn't know what to say. The anger was still there, but it was different now. He wasn't going to hurt anyone. 'I'm sorry for your Mam's window.'

Cerys shrugged. 'I told her it was a stone, a loose stone from the gravel.'

'What, that did all that?'

They were quiet. The smaller models were lit and made little blue-green fires like swamp gas. The crowd oo-ed.

'That's lovely.' Cerys said, looking.

Iestyn still wanted to kiss her. 'I still want to kiss you,' he said.

'No you don't.' She looked at him, flames and reflections of flames in water moving in her eyes. 'Too much trouble. Remember?'

'S'pose so.' Iestyn thought she was probably right.

112

Cerys twisted her fingers together and pushed out her arms stretching her spine, breathing deep. Her finger bones crackled.

'I did – do – really like you, you know. Remember that. That's why I'm not sorry. I'm sorry for after, for all that crying and shouting but I'm not sorry for what really happened. It was worth it. Wasn't it?'

Iestyn stood up. It wouldn't make any difference what he said. He was staying, she was going. She was different from him. She wanted everything.

'Can't you just keep the good bits?' she said.

'Ask me next year.' Iestyn walked away without looking back.

From his jeans pocket he took out an envelope and walked through the crowds towards the huge spiral structure. Tony shouted to him but he hopped over the barrier and across the firebreak and tucked the envelope with her letters and the photos into the firewood.

'Iestyn! Get out of the way.' Tony was carrying a flame thrower and a fire extinguisher. 'I'm supposed to light this up! You've got to get back!'

Iestyn jumped away and felt the heat as Tony lit the big model and a ten-foot curtain of orange flame shot into the air. The crowd aahhed. Iestyn watched as the flame spiralled around and up, the colours intense and compelling. He had to admit the fire looked good.

Up in the dark bowl of the sky Fassbinder-Hurley streaked like a thumbprint smudge past earth. Iestyn watched the fire climbing, and the comet streaking. It wasn't like a picture of a comet at all. It was like the effect you get when you point a video camera at a lightbulb: a blur of moving light. Twenty minutes and it was all over.

Iestyn wasn't sure if he was disappointed. Nothing had changed, no aliens had dropped out of the sky from its tail. It didn't crash-land in the sea. The crowd was clapping and cheering and little kids were waving their glow-in-the-dark sticks. Iestyn felt empty.

The were a couple of film crews, one some mates of Connie's and another from BBC Wales. Iestyn walked over to the silver van and got himself a drink. Tony was being interviewed by a girl with a shaven head. He looked ecstatic. Iestyn watched 'til he'd finished and went over.

'Iestyn, man. What did you think? Excellent or what?'

'Yeah, excellent.'

'I can't wait to see the photos.' He wiped his forehead and took a swig from the bottle in his hand. 'Ah, well. Goodnight Fassbinder-Hurley. Thanks for everything.'

Iestyn said nothing.

'Are you coming to help, tomorrow? It's always a bit of a drag, the clearing up. But it was worth it. Don't you reckon?'

'Yeah.' Iestyn looked over to where Cerys had been. She wasn't there. Gone home early to pack, Iestyn thought. He shrugged. 'S'pose so.'

Iestyn walked through the crowd of comet spotters to the car park. He'd have to see about getting a lift home himself.

'Iestyn! Sorry we're late.' Rich had driven up in his Dad's Land Rover with Martine Lloyd. 'We had to give some of her mates a lift.' He jumped down and unlocked the back.

'Bloody hell, Rich! Smells of sheep in there!'

There was a tall, brown-haired girl wearing a green vest. As she moved towards the light in the car park Iestyn noticed her back covered in freckles and stared.

'That's Rachel,' Rich said, seeing him look. 'Martine's mate. She swims freestyle for Wales.'